The Witches' Bridge

Books by Barbee Oliver Carleton

The Witches' Bridge
Chester Jones
The Secret of Saturday Cove

The Witches' Bridge

by BARBEE OLIVER CARLETON

HOLT, RINEHART AND WINSTON

New York   Chicago   San Francisco

This book is affectionately dedicated
to the boys and girls of
the Brookwood School, Manchester, Mass.,
and to Ann Durell,
with the author's gratitude for
the editor's insight and patience.

CONTENTS

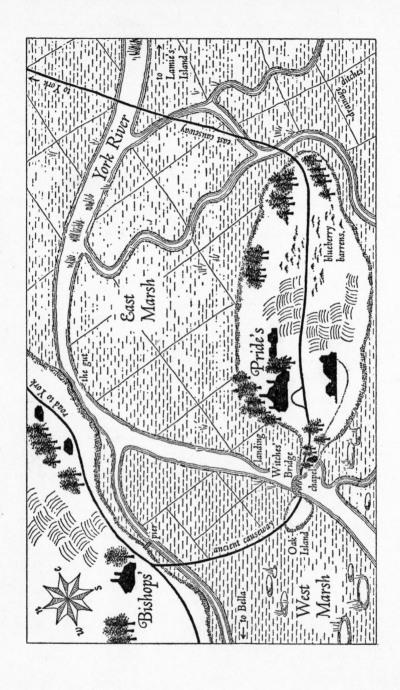

CHAPTER ONE

Young Dan Pride

~~~~~~~~~~~~~~~~~~~~~~~~~~~~~~~~~

THE gray day ended as it began, too cold for May, and threatening a storm. Now the wind swept out of the east, lashing the sea. It drove the tide up through the harbor and past the town, into the great salt marsh beyond.

Here, for half the course of the clock, the sea would invade the land. The black tide, branching and re-branching into its creeks and waterways, would fill and overflow the ancient beds of salt hay. It would hide, for a time, the treacherous salt ponds. Then around midnight the tide would halt, and slowly draw back into the sea.

But all night long the wind and the rain, like powers of darkness, would turn this wasteland into a wild witches' sabbath.

Back in the town the rain began to fall. It streamed against the windshield of the jeep station wagon making its way down Main Street.

Dan Pride wiped the steam from the window and saw his own face, and the anxiety in it. Quickly he made his face go cold and safe. Then he gazed out at the town. His father at thirteen had known these very stores, these great trees, these houses with their fences and lilacs. He tried hard to see his father at his own age—, confident and happy, walking through this town. But he could see only himself minutes ago, climbing down from the Boston bus with his suitcases and his violin, and his face set cold and safe. He could still see the men on the street corner, the watchful men with their sharp features. They had seemed alien, talking among themselves in their strange coastal dialect, and Dan stood apart, unsure of what to do.

It was a lonely wait there on the sidewalk. Then, through the first drops of rain came Billy Ben, like a burst of sunshine. The hired man was ruddy and square, with a big face as friendly as a window.

"Welcome to York, Dan Pride! What's the matter, too proud for the welcome committee?" But his ready laugh with the men was meant for Dan as well.

With mock ceremony he handed the boy into the jeep and threw the luggage into the back with the foreign labels showing. But when he came to the violin his manner changed. "What do you know?" he said softly. "We got ourselves another fiddler!" He pushed the violin behind the suitcases and slammed the door, as if Dan had something to hide.

The men exchanged glances and moved into the store out of the rain. Uneasy, Dan stared after them.

But Billy Ben jumped in with a cheerful shrug and started up the jeep. "Off for Pride's Point!"

"How far is it, please?" asked Dan.

"Twelve miles out in the marsh, the old way." Billy Ben

looked at the boy. "You had any supper? You look used up."

"Yes, thanks, on the plane," Dan told him. The London plane, the last link with his old life, was behind him. What lay ahead he had no means of knowing.

Billy Ben struck up a whistle as if to cheer the tired boy beside him. So they left the town behind and headed inland, past farms and woodlots. But always Dan could glimpse the river, running fast with the tide, and the rain pelting hard onto its surface.

"Well, Dan Pride," his companion said suddenly, "what do you think of our town?"

Dan noticed suddenly that Billy Ben was a young man, still in his twenties. With his sharp brown eyes he would not be readily fooled. "I like what I saw of York. Really," Dan said thinly.

"You like it like poison," laughed Billy Ben. "But I guess York must seem pretty dull after London, and some of those cities you've lived in."

"It isn't that," Dan said quickly. "It's just that the men back there didn't seem—friendly."

Billy Ben shrugged. "No ambition, that's all. They work part time in the shipyard, and spend the rest of the time hanging around town hatching up trouble. You got to plan if you want to get somewhere."

"But it seemed almost as if they didn't like me."

Billy Ben hesitated. "Didn't your daddy ever tell you about the town? About growing up at Pride's Point?"

"No, though I often asked him. I expect he was homesick."

Billy Ben shook his great head. "That wasn't the reason.

Even foreign correspondents talk about home, I guess."
He glanced at Dan. "I'll tell you this much. It isn't you
they don't like. It's who you are. Some folks in town had
just as soon all the Prides cleared out of York, and stayed
out."

In disbelief Dan watched the windshield wipers sweep
back and forth. *Cleared out and stayed out. Cleared out
and stayed out,* said the wipers.

But the Prides were an honorable family. Long ago
they had even settled the town, his mother had told him.
Swiftly his temper rose against those unknown men on the
corner. He turned on Billy Ben. "Why? Why shouldn't
they like the Prides?"

"Small town stuff," said Billy Ben easily. "Prides have
always been standoffish. And then there was something
that happened back in witchcraft times. Most folks in
town don't even know what it was all about. But they
keep ahold of the grudge just the same."

Witchcraft times. Grudge. Dan stared out of the window. So this was why the men had been silent. They resented the Prides for their pride, and for something that
had happened long ago and been forgotten. Wearily he
held to one thought: his Uncle Julian, at least, would have
a welcome for him.

Billy Ben changed the subject. "What you been doing
with yourself, Dan Pride? Tell us about it."

It was a subject which brought Dan no pleasure. But
the man meant to be friendly. So he told a little of his life
in Europe during the happy years which were already
growing hazy.

Billy Ben ran his tongue over his generous lips. "Travel,

that's the thing. Living like a lord in the big cities. You speak all those languages, Dan, boy?"

Dan shook his head. "I didn't live like a lord. And I went mostly to schools where they taught in English."

"You speak different, though. Real British. And then, what?"

Dan went on tonelessly. "After my parents were killed in the plane crash, I went to a boarding school near London. During the holidays I went to camp on the continent. Once I stayed with the family of one of my masters in Paris."

There, it was over. Three years of loneliness explained so often, and always told in these few, empty words. Not a hint of the grief, and the shameful new fears of being unwelcome among "friends", and not being very clever at anything, and being smaller than others his age. No mention of the long hours he had learned to pass in the kinder company of books.

But Billy Ben's eyes were shining enviously. "Pretty special for a thirteen-year-old, I'd say."

Dan looked at the man, surprised at his envy. Billy Ben couldn't know what it was like to be without a home and family.

The jeep bumped on over the dirt road. Outside, the woods gave way to a clutter of sumac and scrub pine. Here and there they passed shacks built close to the road, each with a small boat overturned in the yard. This was a wild area, good for nothing but the bleakest of living.

Dan wondered how much farther they must go before he would be at his uncle's house. It did not matter that he had never met his father's brother Julian. What mattered was that he would have a home again, a family life that might be as happy and loyal as his own had been.

He peered through the rain, eager for his first glimpse of the great salt marshes. "What is Pride's Point like?" he asked curiously.

"It's self-sufficient, like the old places, with its own orchard and gardens and such. And it stays the same while the world keeps changing." Then Billy Ben's voice grew matter-of-fact. "But if I had it, I'd make it different. I'd make it pay me good hard money."

"Does anyone live on the island besides Prides?"

Billy Ben laughed shortly. "Just us Coreys. And I've lived there all my life, except for a spell in York, working at the shipyard. Coreys have always worked for Prides," he added, "and that's a long time. The Prides raised the old house back in Puritan times there above the point, so as to be safe from the Indians. And they've kept themselves to themselves ever since."

Suddenly the wilderness ended, and Dan caught a glimpse of lawns and bright flower beds and a friendly colonial house. Smoke rose from a chimney and lights were glowing cheerfully, though night had not yet fallen. Had they crossed a bridge without his knowing it, and could this be Pride's Point? With a quick hope, Dan turned to Billy Ben.

But Billy Ben shook his head. "That place belongs to the Bishops."

"Are they neighbors of ours?"

"You mean your daddy never told you about the Bishops?"

Dan shook his head.

"Just keep clear of the Bishops."

Why? Dan wanted to ask. But Billy Ben was staring ahead into the rain, and there had been a roughness in his voice like an order. And in that moment Dan saw something strange.

Just beyond the Bishop place, the road turned aside at a ledge. Here, half hidden by the thicket and drenched by the rain, crouched a figure. For an instant the eyes held Dan's, bright with a greeting, or a warning. Then they were past. Dan looked back, uncertain whether he had seen a human figure, or anything at all.

But before he could speak of it, the jeep dipped down an incline and made a sharp turn. Dan stared in wonder. There before them and far beyond stretched the salt marsh. Mile on desolate mile reached abroad into the half-light. In this eerie limbo raged the wind and the rain with nothing to break their fury. And through the whole wild wasteland the creeks went roiling and twisting like bright snakes among the islands.

His eyes dark with dread, Dan looked at Billy Ben. Surely no one would choose to live in such a place! "Did we take the wrong road?"

Billy Ben shook his shaggy head. He threw the jeep into low gear and they started across the marsh. He drove with caution now, following the dim causeway road like a tightrope walker. They seemed to have entered a lost world, vast and bleak, filled with terror.

After an eternity the scene changed. Far ahead Dan saw the dark hump of an island sheared by the river, and across the river another island larger than the first. A stone bridge connecting the two was silhouetted black above the water.

Dan's eyes were drawn to the bridge. It was of ancient

design. With its three strong arches it looked as timeless as the islands which it joined. Somehow the sight filled him with foreboding.

"We call that the Witches' Bridge," announced Billy Ben. "It leads across to Pride's. Folks don't come this way if they can help it, but there's no fog tonight."

Dan wondered fleetingly what difference fog would have made. Then eagerly, he looked toward the larger island with its long point reaching toward them from the headland. Pride's Point! But through the driving rain and the darkness, he could see no light at all. Not yet. The entire island was as black as the bridge ahead.

"Why do they call it the Witches' Bridge?"

Billy Ben said easily, "Old Samuel Pride was a witch."

"A witch!" Dan cried in disbelief.

"Accused, condemned, and executed. Let's see," said Billy Ben, thinking aloud, "he was your great-great-granddaddy's—no. Farther back than that; eleven generations of Prides since Samuel. And back in Puritan times when he built Pride's Point, witchcraft was a crime punishable by death. Don't you know your Bible? 'Thou shalt not suffer a witch to live!' "

"But what proof did they have that he was a witch?"

"Proof enough. If you were different in those days, maybe you were a witch. Old Samuel was high and mighty, and hot-tempered. He hated folks, and he kept to himself. And he could play the fiddle like a wizard."

Dan glanced at Billy Ben. Was there a special meaning in his words?

"Also he had the finest house in York," continued Billy Ben meaningfully, "with several hundred acres of the best marshland."

"They were jealous," Dan put in bitterly.

Billy Ben shrugged. "Could be. Anyway, the neighbors began to say he could fix 'em with his eye, and bad luck would follow them all day. They even claimed that Samuel's fiddling called the Devil out of the marsh in the shape of a great black dog, and then the butter soured in the churn and the cows wandered off and drowned in the salt ponds—"

"That's rot!" snapped Dan. "It was probably hot weather. It would have been only natural for the food to spoil, and the cows to go in search of water!"

Billy Ben chuckled. "You got the Pride temper, even if you are pint-sized."

Dan said nothing. Billy Ben could not know how much he hated being small for his age.

"I bet old Samuel told them the same thing. But it didn't do him any good. They issued a warrant for his arrest and one foggy night they came after him, heading across the marsh with their lanterns, and the Bishops right up at the front—"

The Bishops, Dan remembered. The people he was to "keep clear of."

"He came down to meet them, Bishops and all." The jeep moved onto the bridge and Billy Ben lowered his voice. "Right here on the bridge, Samuel pronounced the curse that some say has never lost its power."

"Does anyone know what the curse was?" Dan asked reluctantly.

"Everyone knows, and for good reason. It goes like this:

'Out of the night, and the fog, and the marsh, these three,

Doom shall come for thee.' "

"Doom?" Dan frowned.

"Fate. An evil fate, like ruin or death. But they took him away and jailed him as a witch, and his wife too, later on."

"They hanged them?"

Billy Ben's face closed and he said briefly, "They tried and hanged Elizabeth. They did worse than that to Samuel."

They were on solid ground again, crossing a causeway onto the point. The boy was glad they had left the grim bridge behind. Pride's Island! They made their way along the narrow point and the wind brawled out of the marsh, reaching after them.

Dan was eager to hear the rest of the story before they arrived at the house. "Did Samuel's curse ever work?"

"That's the queer part of it," said Billy Ben. "Because with the next fog, an epidemic struck the town and took a lot of people. So folks began to believe in the curse. All that happened close to three hundred years ago. But they still say there's something out here in the marsh, something that can't be explained. Signal lights beckoning travelers into the salt ponds. A dog howling, when all the dogs are called in and accounted for. Some claim that when trouble's coming you'll hear Samuel's fiddle, faint and far off. I've sure heard it," he added shortly.

With a sinking heart, Dan saw that Billy Ben was telling the truth.

"When we get a heavy fog around here, we still call it a Fiddler's fog. Folks may laugh it off, but they don't take chances. They stay out of the marsh till the fog lifts."

The jeep snarled upward. The headlights gleamed on two rows of sodden willow trees.

"What happens when someone does hear the Fiddler?" Dan asked.

Billy Ben snorted. "Most times trouble, folks say in town. Either to the poor jinx that heard it, or to somebody else. And they'll give you a dozen stories to prove it."

Dan felt a little chill at his back, as if a door had slowly opened behind him into the night. "But surely people don't believe this?"

The hired man pursed his full lips. "Your granddaddy Dan Pride laughed at the whole thing." The words seemed to imply more than they said.

"What happened?"

Billy Ben glanced at him in surprise. "If your own daddy didn't tell you, I guess it's up to your Uncle Julian."

The tossing willows ended at the top of the rise. For a short space the wind slammed unchecked against the jeep. Then Dan saw the house, a rambling huddle of steep gables and age-blackened walls.

"I'll leave you off here, and go put the car away." Billy Ben stopped the jeep. "Welcome to Pride's Point," he said dryly.

Dan strained to see through the driving rain. The headlights shone on a massive doorway. Some long-dead craftsman had carved a broad coat of arms high on the lintel, and on either side hung great pineapples hewn of wood. The ancient symbol of hospitality, Dan had once read. But no welcoming light brightened the worn entrance. Only through the streaming windows at one side a dim light flickered, as if someone sat alone with only a fire for comfort.

"Your uncle's in the library. Go on in."

Dan hesitated, and Billy Ben nodded in sympathy. "Go on. Just turn right at the hall." The hired man reached past him and opened the door of the jeep.

Dan shot him a glance of gratitude, then ran with pounding heart through the rain. On the threshhold he hesitated, fighting the feeling that he was about to enter a prison.

Then he let himself in and softly pulled the great door shut behind him.

CHAPTER TWO

Mystery

~~~~~~~~~~~~~~~~~~~~~~~~~~~~~~~~~~

DAN stood in a broad hall paneled and furnished in some distant, darker period. Paintings of early Prides hung on the walls and gazed somberly down the staircase. The great newel, Dan saw, was carved with the same coat of arms which loomed above the lintel outside.

Eager, yet fearful of meeting the uncle whom he had never seen, the boy started toward the library. Something, a sound on the stairs, caused him to glance up. A figure lurked motionless just beyond the landing. Surely it was the form of a great dog, the squat head thrust forward, the evil gaze steady on his own. A black dog. Sharply, Dan drew in his breath.

The shape turned and disappeared into the dimness above. Dan's heart hammered against his ribs. What had Billy Ben said? That Samuel Pride with his violin had summoned the Devil out of the marsh in the shape of a great black dog!

Despising his dread, Dan moved swiftly to the staircase. But there was nothing on the landing except a case clock, ticking loudly.

A voice called from the library. "Is that you, Billy Ben? Bring the boy in here." It was a cultured voice, one to be respected. Yet it was weak like a sick man's. Dan hurried into the library, and stopped.

The man seated by the fire gazed back at him with the hollow eyes of a death's head. His face must once have been a handsome one: the nose was bold and the brow high and scholarly. But now it seemed forbidding, so bitter and lined it was. With a sinking heart, Dan saw not even the pretense of a welcome.

Then his uncle smiled, a grimace that quickly fled and left his face more haunted than before. "So Billy Ben sent you in alone to Pride's Point."

"How do you do, sir." Dan went forward to take his uncle's hand. The flesh felt as cold as death. He wondered how he could ever bring himself to call this man Uncle Julian.

"Sit down, Dan."

Dan sat, and hid his thoughts, enduring his kinsman's scrutiny. Slowly his dream of a happy home at Pride's Point flickered and went out.

Finally his uncle nodded. "Your father was right to go away. But a whole generation lost to Pride's Point—" He sighed deeply, as if he were alone in the dim room. " 'Hatred. It's a disease to run away from,' I told your father. 'There are too many hiding places at Pride's, and there's too much hidden.' That's what I told him the night he left."

Hiding places. Hatred. What hatred had his father

turned his back on? What things were hidden? Perhaps if he made no move, no reply, his uncle would tell him.

Abruptly the low voice became strong. The dull eyes flared into life. "I hope to Heaven I haven't done wrong to bring you here!"

"Oh no, sir," Dan cried. "I'm sure I'll get to like it here!"

"I was not thinking merely of whether you will like it," his uncle said, and Dan felt the blood burn into his face. "Pride's Point is no place for a boy. This is why I have waited so long before sending for you. Also, I am fixed in my habits, and there is only Mrs. Corey—and Billy Ben— to do for us. Now that you are here, certain things will have to change."

His uncle rose and poked absently at the fire. Dan tried not to think how all this differed from his thoughts of homecoming. Stoically, he stared around the room. The library was long and narrow, dark-paneled from floor to ceiling and dominated by the largest fireplace Dan had ever seen. The fire was generous, welcome in such wild weather. But on this mammoth hearth it seemed forlorn.

"I have my work to do," his uncle said frowning. "You must not count on me for company. But you will make friends. I have seen youngsters your age around those small houses across the marsh."

"Yes, sir," said Dan.

"Mrs. Corey will see you in the morning about your meals and laundry and such things. Billy Ben will ask you to perform certain chores. Also, your headmaster informs me that you plan to study in your free time."

"Yes, sir," said Dan, swept along miserably in the chill current of his uncle's words.

Julian Pride looked at him sharply. "Have you eaten, Dan?"

"Yes, thank you. On the plane." Unaccountably, Dan's throat tightened.

"You're tired, aren't you?"

Dan nodded. Suddenly the tall man by the fire was his dead father. In a moment he would surely laugh his wonderful laugh, and take his quick step forward to roughen Dan's hair.

A door slammed, and the moment passed. His uncle turned wearily back to the fire. Like the town of York, his uncle did not want him here.

There was a soft whistling and Billy Ben stood in the doorway with Dan's bags beside him. "You should have the lights on, sir," he said with concern. "It isn't—good for you to sit alone in the dark."

His uncle did not answer. He said tonelessly, "Billy Ben will show you to your room. Goodnight, Dan."

Dan paused at the door. How did one give thanks to a man whose help had been offered unwillingly? He said in a thin voice, "Thank you, sir."

But Julian Pride was shifting a log on the hearth. He did not hear. He seemed to have returned to some other world of his own.

Dan took up a bag and followed Billy Ben. He was depressed and thoughtful. What was the reason for his uncle's wretchedness? The tragedies of the past? The old house itself, perhaps, brooding and sinister as it was? Or could it be that Julian, like Samuel Pride the witch, resented not only the Bishops but everyone around him— even young Dan Pride, a boy whom he did not want?

They moved on into a steep-gabled wing of the main house. This wing, Billy Ben pointed out, was the original house built by Samuel. There was a feeling of great age about the place which the night light, burning lonesomely in the hall, did nothing to lighten.

Billy Ben began to whistle. "Danny Boy". It was a plaintive air, one which Dan had often played on the violin, always with tenderness. The hired man whistled it jauntily, and the effect was disquieting, false.

Down three steep steps and along a drafty passageway like a whistling Pied Piper went Billy Ben. Finally he stopped before a narrow door, flung it open, and snapped on a light. "Here you are, Danny Boy."

It was a small room in a gable. Against its leaded windows the storm hammered for admittance. But here inside, someone had made an attempt at coziness. There was a spool bed spread with a gay quilt. A ship model surmounted the small chest. The desk was equipped with a student's lamp, and well-worn books filled the bookcase. The plastered walls were bare, but the floor was covered with a bright rug, and on the grate a fire lay ready to be lighted.

Dan's hopes rose. "Did my uncle do this?"

"Not him. Mrs. Corey fixed it up last week, grumbling her head off as usual."

Dan turned away.

Billy Ben said heartily, "Don't you mind being off by yourself here. You'll get used to it. Anyway, you have the best view of the Witches' Bridge in the whole place." He waved goodnight. Then his steps struck lightly against the old floor boards and echoed down the passage.

The silence fell like a blanket. Dan hurried in panic into the passageway after Billy Ben. Then, ashamed, he firmly closed the door. "Just make the best of things," his father used to say. Well, he had reached his journey's end and here at Pride's Point, wanted or not, he would make the best of things. He would start by putting away his belongings. He would not think about the welcome he had hoped for and the family he had dreamed about.

Dan took his violin out of its case. If only he dared play it he could rid himself of much of the pain within him. Then he remembered Billy Ben's strange reaction to the violin in York. He replaced the instrument and stored it well back in the closet.

He unpacked his suitcases, making the task last as long as possible. He arranged neatly on the chest the set of brushes which his mother had given him one Christmas, along with the last picture taken of his parents. Then he gazed around the room. It did not look like home. It looked like a room set up apart from the rest of the household for a boy without a home.

And there was a sense of foreboding, of mystery, about it. The oaken beams, the deep windows, the age-black paneling—these were his roots. Yet he was a stranger to all this. Unwanted. With the loneliness, the worries returned: he was small, unskillful, secretly afraid of things.

Dan remembered with some nostalgia his bare room at the Governor School in England. He remembered the comforting hum of traffic. He went to the window, and the memory fled. Outside the wind raged and the rain beat hard at the pane. Close to the point he made out the pale loop of the river. And there, there was the ancient bridge, crouching black above it.

Dan whispered to himself,

" 'Out of the night, and the fog, and the marsh, these three,

Doom shall come for thee.' "

Then he stiffened. In the distance he heard the howling of a dog! He listened, not breathing, and the rain drove in on him unnoticed.

Then Dan narrowed his eyes. Had he seen a light out there in the marsh? He stared into the blackness until his eyes shifted in their sockets. Yes! There it came. The light winked again, and yet again. With a thrill of relief Dan realized that it was flashing a signal. No will-o'-the-wisp would be sending the Morse Code, which he remembered from his camp days on the continent!

It flashed steady and slow. Dan had little difficulty in following it. "D-A-N—DAN PRIDE—" said the light.

Then it stopped. Dan waited, shivering wet at the window. He waited until he was stiff and sore, and the rain began to lessen.

But the great marsh remained dark. The wind ripped and tore at the clouds, showing the clear, vast night beyond.

CHAPTER THREE

The Witch's Curse

~~~~~~

THE sun at mid-morning entered the gable room and streamed across the bed. Dan felt it, warm and comforting, on his eyelids. Then he remembered his strange homecoming: the stormy night just past, the light signaling his name in the marsh, the weird howling of the dog. His eyes flew open and, defensive, he sprang out of bed.

But in the daylight his room had taken on a different character. Now it seemed friendly, even homelike.

Dan gazed down past the clustered black roofs beyond his gable. Hundreds of daffodils dotted the field across from the giant beeches. Perhaps, three hundred years ago, Samuel Pride himself had planted them both, homesick for the English countryside he had left behind.

Dan glanced at his clock and saw that he had overslept, for it had been late last night before he finally fell asleep. Hurriedly he bathed and dressed. Swiftly he tidied his room, as he had been expected to do at Governor.

But now that he was ready to go, to become part of this

strange new home for the first time, he hesitated. His uncle would have no wish to see him. And the house-keeper, Mrs. Corey, would be annoyed because of the extra work. He must eat breakfast as quickly as possible, thought Dan, and then he would go in search of Billy Ben. He hurried out of the old passageway into the main house and on down the stairs.

What had looked last night like the shape of a black dog was, he decided scornfully, merely the shadow cast by the case clock on the landing. He moved without a sound past the library.

A carved door opened from the hall into a dining room, low-beamed and long. Here were the same somber fur-nishings, the same dark paneling which he had seen in the library. But this great hearth was bright with copper bric-a-brac, and white curtains softened the windows. Flower-ing plants, too, showed that here a woman had been al-lowed a free hand.

On the wall above the great table was a portrait that stopped Dan in his tracks. It was his Uncle Julian, surely, in the stern costume of a Puritan. Here was the same proud nose and brow, the same sharp angles of cheekbone and jaw. Only the eyes differed. The painted eyes were commanding and arrogant. They seemed to fix Dan with some message of their own as he moved uneasily into the kitchen.

A stout, heavy-browed woman came out of the pantry carrying a pitcher of milk and a pot of jam.

"Good morning, Dan Pride," said she, as matter-of-fact as if she had known him all her life. "Want your breakfast in the dining room, or over there?"

"Over there" was a sunny breakfast bay which overlooked the eastern side of Pride's Island opposite the Witches' Bridge.

"Over there is fine," said Dan. "You must be Mrs. Corey."

"That's right." The woman's voice was curt, but her manner was kind enough as she hurried breakfast before him. Then she sat down to the task of polishing the silver which Dan's arrival had interrupted.

He said awkwardly, "Thank you for fixing my room."

"That's the least anyone could do," she sniffed.

The boy flushed. It must be well known at Pride's Point that Dan's uncle had sent for him merely out of a sense of duty.

Over Mrs. Corey's graying head an ancient wag-on-the-wall clock ticked irregularly. Dan toyed with the scrambled eggs and broiled ham, aware of their excellence and wishing he felt hungrier.

"How'd you sleep?" the housekeeper asked abruptly.

"Very well, thank you. Once I got to sleep."

"Wind blew hard last night," she commented. "It's hard sleeping at Pride's Point when the wind blows. And it blows most of the time, here in the marsh."

Dan looked out. It was blowing a little now, rippling the river where it curved through the marsh beyond a slope of orchard.

"Something besides the wind kept me awake last night," he said carefully. "I heard a dog howling. And I thought I saw a light signaling, out in the marsh."

Mrs. Corey dropped a large soup ladle. It made a terrible clatter and the color left her broad face. Yet as Dan picked it up for her he could not see that it was damaged in any way.

"Where'd the light come from?" asked Mrs. Corey after a moment.

Dan thought. "It seemed to come from beyond the old bridge, the one they call the Witches' Bridge."

Mrs. Corey laid down the piece of silver and said in a low voice, "Listen to me, Dan Pride. You keep away from the marsh at night, 'specially when it's foggy, hear me? Don't you ever go near it!"

Dan nodded, wondering at her intensity. "Billy Ben told me about Samuel Pride the witch, and his curse—that evil will come out of the marsh on a foggy night. Is that what you mean?"

"Just you do as I say." The housekeeper clamped her mouth shut and polished the ladle as if life itself depended on the sheen she gave it.

"Mrs. Corey," Dan said tentatively, "What happened to my grandfather?"

But the woman was on her guard now. "If you want to know such things, you ask your uncle."

Dan thought briefly about his uncle's aloofness, the bitterness in his eyes. "I'm afraid he wouldn't tell me. And possibly I should know."

Back and forth, round and round, went the polishing cloth. A deep line appeared between Mrs. Corey's brows. "Your Uncle Julian wants to forget about these things. He doesn't forget, though. These things have been eating him up for years. More so, the older he grows."

Dan ate very quietly. Perhaps now he would learn the reason for his uncle's wretchedness.

"You better hear what happened, no matter what any-one says." Mrs. Corey spoke rapidly as if she meant to get it over with. "You've heard then, about Samuel Pride the witch. And his curse."

Dan nodded.

"Well, long before your grandpa's time the Prides had believed in that curse, like everyone else. And they had reason."

Dan nodded. Billy Ben had said the same thing. "But what about my grandfather?"

Mrs. Corey shook her head. "Didn't hold with it. All superstitious twaddle, he used to say. He was writing a book on the family history, all about Samuel's case, and the legend of the curse, and the rest of it. He aimed to prove to folks that when things went wrong it was just chance, didn't have a thing to do with any witch's curse."

Dan set his glass down softly and waited.

"Old Daniel Pride," mused Mrs. Corey. "Trouble was, he didn't know what he was talking about, Lord rest his soul."

"Did you know my grandfather?"

"Saw him around. My cousin, Elder Corey—that's Billy Ben's pa—used to work for him. They lived in the cottage where Billy Ben lives now, out beyond the big barn."

Through the window, Dan could see a little low cottage with deep-set windows and thick stone walls.

"Pride's was more of a farm then, with several hands to do the work, and Elder had full charge of things for your grandpa."

"My grandfather must have had a lot of faith in him," said Dan politely.

"Coreys have always worked for Prides," said the housekeeper, as if this were enough. "Well, the old gentleman tried hard to change things at Pride's Point. He modernized some, and he did other things, too. He owned and played the first violin a Pride ever had since old Samuel. And he always used the old road over the bridge and laughed at us folks who wouldn't." She pointed. "There's the road everyone uses."

Dan looked toward the sun. There the great East Marsh spread out lush and vast and as flat as a floor. A long straight causeway slashed across it to the mainland in the distance.

"We call that the new road, but 'tisn't much newer than the old one. Not long after they took Samuel and Elizabeth away, folks began to shun the bridge. Maybe their consciences bothered them, or maybe they was a-scared of the curse Samuel put on 'em. Anyway, they made a new road to the east, said it was shorter to Boston that way. Samuel's son, Hugh, had the old causeway repaired for the Prides. But I guess they never used it either, unless they couldn't help themselves. Not till your grandpa's time, anyway. And your grandpa wouldn't use anything *but* the old road."

"I should have liked him," said Dan, smiling.

"Most everyone did, but he just wasn't smart. He'd take long walks in the marsh, day *and* night, all sorts of weather. And at the end he was even trying to wipe out the old feud with the Bishops. A turrible mistake." Mrs. Corey shook her head.

"Did the quarrel last all that time?" Dan broke in. "Ever since witchcraft days?"

"It did." Mrs. Corey polished grimly. "The stories I've heard my mother tell! But Prides always hated Bishops worst, and they had reason. It was the Bishops started the whole thing in the first place, about the Prides being witches. It cost Samuel and Elizabeth their lives, and would of cost them Pride's Point, too, except for what Samuel did."

Dan wondered what Samuel had done to save his home, but the housekeeper swept on, caught up by her story.

"Every generation after that there was trouble, one thing or another, between the two families. Prides never said much, they was always proud and offish. But the Bishops talked around a lot and kept folks thinking the Prides was queer. Maybe that's why Prides got to be even more offish. And then your grandpa came along, fed to the teeth with this feud business."

Mrs. Corey laid down her polishing cloth. "Now you listen to what happened. It was about this time of year. Your grandpa went to see Philip Bishop about the shipyard that the Prides once owned. He meant to buy it back into the family for his sons. Philip Bishop was willing to sell, not having any sons to leave it to, just a daughter. And the feud was over, as far as your grandpa was concerned.

"Well, sir, it had been coming in thick all day. By the time your grandpa left the house 'twas a regular Fiddler's fog. He shouldn't of walked in the first place, what with his bad heart. But he started out afoot, heading over the old bridge to the Bishops'. He had his briefcase along, just like always when he had business to do. Only this," she said accusingly, "was business with the Bishops!"

"Go on," said Dan.

"That was the last anyone ever saw him alive!"

Dan felt cold horror spread over him. "But what happened?"

"Nobody knows what happened. The boys took it hard. Your pa was still in college, about to graduate. But your Uncle Julian was an up-and-coming young lawyer then, home from Boston for the weekend. He was the one found the poor gentleman, lying dead near the old chapel down there on the point. They saw the print of his briefcase real clear in the mud, but no briefcase anywhere. And they found his footprints, running, as if somebody or something was after him and he'd tried to get home from the marsh."

Dan refused to believe what Mrs. Corey was suggesting. "But he had a bad heart, you say. Possibly that's all there was to it."

Mrs. Corey looked at him. "Then why the running footprints? And what happened to that briefcase?"

Dan was silent.

"And there was something else, too. Folks on the mainland remembered seeing queer lights out in the marsh. And Elder Corey, down to his cottage, heard a fiddle that night and thought it was your grandpa playing. But all the time there was the poor old gentleman lying down there on the point, with a turrible look on him, so they said." The housekeeper's eyes were back on her work, but genuine fear was written on her face.

"Did they ever find the briefcase?" Dan prompted.

Mrs. Corey shook her head. "Never, though your uncle and your pa most tore the place apart. So did Billy Ben when he came back to work here after has pa died."

Memory stirred in Dan like a chill wind. "There are too many hiding places in Pride's Point," Uncle Julian had once said to his father. "And too much hidden."

"What was in the briefcase?" Dan demanded.

"Papers, I suppose, to prove he'd bought the shipyard. But since the old gentleman was dead, and the papers lost, Philip Bishop and his daughter Ann swore he never bought it at all. That's the Bishops for you!"

Bishops! Dan felt a sharp resentment at the name.

"It's not my place to say, but *I* can tell you where that briefcase is." The housekeeper paused dramatically.

"Where?" asked Dan.

"If you ask me, that briefcase is at the bottom of the big salt pond out in the West Marsh, the one that looks like an evil eye. Bella, they call it. And no human hand threw it in there, either. *I* don't have to guess what old Dan was running from, what with that look on his face. He'd laughed at Samuel's curse, and he'd had dealings with the Bishops. So what else could happen?"

Round and round again went the polishing cloth, back and forth.

"Then the talk started up worse than ever, spite of all your grandpa had tried to do to stop such talk. The night and the fog and the marsh, and Elder Corey hearing the Fiddler—and then doom, for old Mr. Dan himself. He wasn't so smart after all. He should of left things alone."

Mrs. Corey frowned out of the window at the bright May morning. "Pride's Point has a bad name in town and it's rubbed off on your Uncle Julian. Why, some folks look at him as if they was even a-scared he'd put the evil eye on 'em."

Pity stirred in Dan for his uncle. To be feared for no

reason— "But Prides never brought bad luck to anyone—
except themselves," he said. "It was the Bishops!"

"Maybe," said Mrs. Corey. "But if you ask me, that's
why your pa went away—to get clear of the whole thing,
and try to forget about it. All this has been like a blight on
the Prides."

Dan brooded. Mrs. Corey was right. That was exactly
how his uncle looked—like a blighted plant, doomed even
while it lived.

Then he had a thought. "But why didn't Uncle Julian,
like his father, try to be friendly with the Bishops?"

Mrs. Corey said slowly, "He always *said* he doesn't believe the Fiddler had anything to do with his father's
trouble. But he believes the Bishops did!"

"The Bishops!"

Mrs. Corey nodded firmly. "And he's never stopped hat-
ing them for a minute. If you ask me, he knows something
he's not telling."

"About the Bishops?" asked Dan.

"That's a fact. Still—" Mrs. Corey paused, frowning.
"Many's the time these last few years, I've watched him
listen on a foggy night. Listen hard, as if there's something evil out there and he's coming to know it. Not evil
men like the Bishops," she added. "Something worse.
Something unnatural."

Dan found himself looking out toward the marsh, sun-
drenched and secretive. The clock on the wall filled the
silence with its homely *tick*-tack, *tick*-tack, *tick*-tack.

Mrs. Corey scraped back her chair and bore the tray of
silver to the sink. "Your Uncle Julian goes to Boston only
once or twice a week these days, he's gone that far into
himself, and the rest of the time he shuts himself off in the

office here. So I guess it's up to me to lay down the law. You poke around in the marsh all you please in the daylight. But after dark, 'specially when it's foggy, you steer clear of the marsh. Curse or no curse, there's no use tempting fate!"

Dan attempted a laugh as he carried his dishes to the shelf. "Don't worry, Mrs. Corey. No one could hire me to go near that marsh, night or day."

"Living here, you'll go soon enough," she told him dryly. "No place else to go. Only keep an eye out for the salt ponds and the honey pots."

Dan smiled. "What are salt ponds and honey pots?"

"Big and little trouble. Billy Ben'll show you."

Through the window they saw Billy Ben moving in his quick way from one part of the garden to another.

A faint pleasure showed for the first time in the housekeeper's face. "Billy Ben's always busy. Walks just like his pa, fast and light. If your Uncle Julian doesn't find plenty of work for him, Billy Ben'll find it for himself, taking down the old sheds, or digging drains for the gardens, or fixing the foundations. Fact is, he works hardest when your uncle isn't even home." She glanced at the clock. "Go on out now and give him a hand. Lunch is at one. Be on time and washed, even when your uncle isn't here. Which he won't be today till dinnertime."

So his uncle was not at Pride's today. Apparently the housekeeper guessed that Julian Pride did not share his plans with his nephew. Dan managed a smile and thanked her at the door.

Mrs. Corey acknowledged neither smile nor thanks. Drawing her dark brows together, she went noisily about her work as if she had wasted altogether too much time.

CHAPTER FOUR

Pride's Point

~~~~~~

It was a dark story which the housekeeper had told Dan, yet he left the house feeling comforted. Mrs. Corey was forbidding certainly, and superstitious. But Dan felt sure that she, at least, felt some concern for him.

The old house rose behind him with its steep-pitched roofs and its somber gables. What violent deeds, what fears and hatreds Pride's Point had seen! He knew now of the doom which had come to his grandfather out of the marsh by night. And he knew whom his uncle hated so bitterly, and why. But did he know the whole reason for his uncle's withdrawal? Certainly Julian Pride hated the Bishops fanatically because he thought them responsible for his father's death. But was he also coming to believe in some evil force surrounding the Prides? Dan shuddered, and moved away from the chill shadow of the house.

Then he remembered that he had not once asked Mrs. Corey about his own mysteries. Again he heard the demon howl of a dog in the night. He saw again the code, surely flashed by some human hand across the storm-swept marsh. Billy Ben would have the answers.

The hired man was nowhere in sight, but his handiwork was everywhere: in the rich lawns and garden plots, in the neat hedgerows of white lilac that followed the stone walls. Dan looked about helplessly until he heard the whir of a power tool. Eagerly he made his way past the great haycocks in the barnyard to a workshop.

"Come on in," called Billy Ben from the dimness inside. "Better late than never!"

Dan entered, sure of his welcome. Billy Ben had been looking for him. "I overslept. I didn't get to sleep right off last night."

"What's the matter? Strange bed?" Billy Ben was tinkering with a large power mower. He did not look up as Dan told about hearing the dog howl, and seeing the signal light in the marsh. Somehow, here in the workshop, both stories sounded silly.

But Billy Ben did not laugh. He looked grave and shook his head. "No code operators, not around here." Then he said with a lightness which Dan was certain he did not feel, "You just dreamed you heard that howl and saw those lights. We'd been talking about things in the marsh, and you dreamed the whole thing." He added jokingly, "There's something out there, Danny Boy, waiting to get you!"

Dan smiled. Yet he was sure that Billy Ben was truly concerned. With this knowledge, Dan's anxiety began to grow swiftly, like a nightmare, here in the dimness of the workshop. For there *was* something out there, waiting . . .

He was relieved when the hired man pushed the mower outside into the sunlight.

"You good for a short job today?" Billy Ben asked.

"Oh, yes!" cried Dan. He would show Billy Ben how quickly he could fit into life at Pride's Point. He would work hard and well. In time, even his Uncle Julian would be glad he came.

"Ever use a power mower?"

Regretfully, Dan shook his head.

Billy Ben made a series of motions which ended in a short burst of power from the mower. "She starts easy. If you have any trouble, sing out. I'll be in the workshop."

Confidently Dan turned to the mower. The rope proved surprisingly difficult to pull and he worked stubbornly over it. But his efforts got him nowhere. The motor remained silent. Panting, Dan sat back on his heels. The mower seemed to be defying him, like something possessed of a life of its own.

Dan's temper rose hotly, but he determined not to bother Billy Ben. He flew into a furious attack on the starter rope. Nothing. Not even a weak cough. Finally Dan stopped, exhausted and miserable, unable to think of a single false move he had made. Pride's Point itself seemed out to prove that he had no place here, that he was useless as well as unwanted.

Suddenly Billy Ben stood over him in his green shirt and pants, blending with sunshine and shadow. Dan thought briefly that you were not aware of Billy Ben until he stood beside you.

"Didn't you remember to choke her?" He turned a lever

and the mower roared into noisy life. Dan felt sick with shame.

"Let's forget the lawn," Billy Ben said in his great voice. "I'll do it myself when I get to it."

"But I can handle the mower. I'm sure I can!" Dan protested.

"If you really want to do something, go to work with the clippers. They're in the tool shed. Just clip around those beech trees." He pursed his full lips. "You know clippers, Dan?"

Dan nodded and escaped into the tool shed.

A battery of garden implements, rakes, spades, picks, edgers, hung neatly from one wall. From another hung tools less often used, with here and there an ancient horseshoe. There were no clippers in either place. Humiliation began to dull Dan's eagerness to prove that he was worth his salt. Was he not even able to find a pair of common grass clippers? They must be here somewhere, Billy Ben had said they were! Again, desperate, Dan scanned the equipment. No clippers.

"Right in front of you, Danny Boy," Billy Ben's voice held a note of strained patience. He pointed to a shelf behind the rakes. In one of the cubbyholes were several clippers of varying sizes.

"Thanks," Dan muttered. Without looking at Billy Ben he hurried out into the sunshine and got to work. He clipped viciously at the grass as if to make up for his stupidity. Before the task was half done, the muscles in his back were stabbed with hot cramps and his right hand felt like fire.

Stiffly, he released his fingers from the grips. Whole

areas of his palm lay open, red and raw. It would be some time, he thought wryly, before that hand could hold a violin bow. Anyway, he was making his mark on Pride's Point. Even in this small way, his being here did mean something after all! Wincing, he wrapped his handkerchief around his hand and continued. The never-ending minutes dragged on.

Only when the screen door on the workshop slammed, ages later, Dan straightened painfully.

"Good enough," said Billy Ben. But Dan saw that his sharp eyes were not on the clipping which Dan had already done, but rather on the unclipped edge of lawn stretching beyond the beeches. "You'll speed up some with practice," said Billy Ben with false heartiness. "Now how about lunch?"

The thought of food made Dan's stomach lurch. But he forced himself to move, trying to hide the stiffness of his limbs. Slowly, he followed Billy Ben to the house.

The hired man turned at the door. "You put away the clippers? My daddy always said the job isn't done till you put away your tools."

Dan made a lame apology. Turning back, he caught the disappointment in Billy Ben's eyes. His defeat was final. If he could not perform even the simplest task, how could he hope to win Billy Ben's respect? And if he could not win the respect of a kindly hired man, then how could he look for affection from Uncle Julian—morose and remote as he was?

When Dan finally entered the kitchen, Billy Ben was already eating at the kitchen table. Mrs. Corey glanced at the clock. "Lucky your uncle's not here for lunch. Wash up. You'll have yours in the dining room."

Dan was relieved that his uncle had not returned, for their meals together would surely be gloomy, even painful. But when he saw the single place laid for him at the end of the long table, he felt a sudden wave of loneliness. He returned to the kitchen. "Please, Mrs. Corey, may I have lunch here with you and Billy Ben?"

The housekeeper hesitated.

"Prides," declared Billy Ben half-joking, "eat in the dining room, not the kitchen. That's one of the penalties for being a Pride, Danny Boy. Right, Amy?"

Mrs. Corey said nothing. Dan thought guiltily of breakfast that morning in the kitchen. Then he retreated into the dining room and sat forlornly at the foot of the table, sure of Billy Ben's secret scorn. He forced down some food, while Mrs. Corey and her kinsman chatted in the kitchen. Now and then they laughed together. Their companionship nearby made Dan feel more desolate than ever. He hoped an afternoon with his books would pass swiftly, and even found himself looking forward to his uncle's return.

"I have a lot of studying to do," he would say to Billy Ben. He need not make a fool of himself again.

Suddenly the door was thrust open and there stood the hired man, his broad smile teasing. "Well, Dan, my lord, what great eggs are you hatching for the afternoon?"

"None at all," said Dan, his excuse forgotten.

"Then let's have a look around Pride's Point. I'm busier than a pup with fleas, but I guess we can snatch a few minutes."

Gladly Dan jumped up, ready to go.

Billy Ben pointed to Dan's half-finished lunch. "Amy'll chew me out if I hustle you away from that good food. She says you look pindling, like a good east wind'd blow you away."

Dan bolted his lunch, wishing passionately that he were not smaller than other boys his age. Pindling. He felt annoyed with Mrs. Corey. He found himself yearning for Billy Ben's respect even more than for his Uncle Julian's.

As they went out, Mrs. Corey called, "You be sure to show Dan those salt ponds."

Dan's companion laughed with hearty good humor. "Amy, you got salt ponds on the brain. No bright kid of thirteen is going to fall into any salt pond."

Bright. Billy Ben had said *bright*.

Mrs. Corey scowled. "In this house, I wouldn't be too sure of anything!"

Billy Ben winked at Dan. "Salt ponds it is," he said agreeably.

He led the way down the road toward the willows and across a high field which gave into an orchard sloping to the marsh.

"Look there," said Billy Ben, pointing. "See those ditches?"

Dan looked. The marsh spread far and green under the afternoon sun, and through it wound the river, blinding bright. Then he nodded with interest. He saw many straight lines of water running from mainland and island, and emptying into the river, cutting the marshland into great, uneven rectangles. Few lines in nature, Dan knew, are straight. These, then, must be the ditches, man-made in this wilderness of half sea and half land.

"But what are they for?" he asked.

"Drainage, so we can harvest a couple of good crops of salt hay each year."

"Did you make them?" Dan asked curiously.

Billy Ben shook his great head. "We keep 'em from filling in, though. Most of these drains were cut in the seventeenth century, when the only open land was these marshes. Everything else was woods. So the planters who owned marshland were rich: they had fish and waterfowl, and the marsh hay gave 'em feed for their critters and mulch for their Injun corn and thatch for their roofs. All they had to do was ditch the marsh into beds to drain off the sea at low tide. Then they cut the hay at the low run of tides in August, and piled it in stacks on the staddles."

"Staddles?" asked Dan.

"See those circles down there?"

Dan nodded. Here and there across the entire salt marsh strange gray stakes were set in circles. They reminded him of the prehistoric "fairy rings" of rocks made by the ancients on the English moors.

"They look little from here. But they're four foot cedar posts pounded into the turf above the reach of the peak tides. Each circle is several feet across. They used to stack salt hay on 'em till the marsh froze over. Then they fetched it in for the winter with a sledge and team."

Dan's eyes shone. "Do they still do that?"

Billy Ben snorted. "I should hope not. Too slow. Today we use the tractor and bale the hay right on the marsh. There aren't many folks left who cut salt hay, so what we don't use we sell at a profit. Take a look." Billy Ben pointed.

The great East Marsh spread to the horizon, a vast tract

of green and gold, veined with waterways as blue as the sky.

"All that's money, Dan Boy. We'll have a good crop this year. Maybe two, if we hustle." Dan caught the tone of impatience. The marsh was not a wasteland to Billy Ben. It was a place to be used, to be turned into profit.

Then an odd note crept into his voice. "But the Prides have let the West Marsh go. Over there by the bridge the marsh has gone wild for years. The ditches are filling in and the water backs up into the hay beds and can't drain off. Then the beds rot out and salt ponds form."

Dan pricked up his ears. "Salt ponds?"

"Miserable things. Like the honey pots, only bigger. You get into one of those old ponds and you go straight down to China. They fool you. From here they look like nice little pools. But they're filled with black stagnant water, and the biggest ones are like bottomless pits."

Dan squinted toward the Witches' Bridge. Beyond it, circles of water dotted the marsh, innocent-looking and bright. They ranged in size from big puddles to small ponds. One, much larger than the others, almost filled a rotted bed far to the west.

"That big one even has a name," said Billy Ben. "We call her Bella."

Mrs. Corey had spoken of Bella. Dan asked tightly, "What if you get into a salt pond and can't swim?"

Billy Ben laughed heartily as if Dan had just told a good joke. "If you can't swim and you get into one of those, your troubles are over."

"Then isn't it awfully dangerous to go out into the marsh there where the salt ponds are?"

"You can see 'em, can't you? You don't have to head into 'em."

"But what if it's dark?" Dan persisted. "Or foggy?"

Billy Ben shrugged. "Nobody goes there when it's dark—or foggy." He said suddenly, "Can you swim, Danny Boy?"

Dan hesitated. Swimming had been required by the camp which he had attended in Germany one summer. It had been taught by an unpleasant little man, and Dan had hated it. By the end of the season, he had barely passed the minimum requirements.

"Well, only a little," he said finally.

"Good! You'll have plenty of chance to practice here," said Billy Ben cheerfully. He nodded toward the swift blind waters of the river.

Dan eyed the marsh with new dismay.

"There's an old skiff up at the barn. I'll help you patch her up. That'll give you a way to get out of here and poke around on your own. Just keep an eye out for Lamie," Billy Ben added.

"Lamie?"

Billy Ben tapped his forehead. "You'll hear about Lamie soon enough!" He glanced at his watch. "Back to work for me. But you look around. Just show up in time for dinner at seven. Your loving uncle won't be kept waiting." A sympathetic wink, and Billy Ben went whistling across the field.

Wistfully Dan watched the cheery form disappear into the shadow of the beeches. Billy Ben loved Pride's Point, and he had enjoyed showing him the place, Dan was sure of it. If Dan did his part, they might even become friends.

Slowly turning, the boy surveyed his new world. Pride's Island was a strong little prison, bounded by a vast and frightening moat of salt marsh. Dan felt like turning tail and fleeing from the vastness into his room. But Billy Ben would surely be keeping an eye on him. There was nothing for it but to go forth and explore—anywhere but in the marsh, Dan resolved firmly.

Where should he go first? He looked upon the broad fields, the sloping orchard, a noble stand of spruce beyond the blueberry barrens. Spring flowers dotted the open spaces of the island, and the fruit trees were bouquets of pink and white against the blue sky. Reluctantly, Dan admitted to himself that he had rarely seen a place of such perfect beauty. He imagined his father, a young man, saying goodby to all this. It could not have been easy. He turned back full circle and his heart leaped in hope. Perhaps he could avoid exploring the island after all, since Billy Ben was returning across the field. He had something in his hand.

"Your swim trunks," he grinned. "You'll get hot, poking around the marsh. The best place to swim, later on, is down there in the East Marsh by the Gut. See where the river narrows? It's fast, but safe enough for a baby. Besides, I'll have an eye on you." A friendly wave and he was off again, a green, living part of Pride's Point.

Safe enough for a baby. With heavy steps, Dan headed the other way, down the road between the willows. The gravel rolled beneath his feet, making his footing unsure. What would it be like on the marsh? Did one sink down into it? Did one follow, or avoid, the swift creeks? Were the salt ponds hidden by dead grass so that they might form a trap for the stranger? Dan wished fervently that Billy Ben were with him. Then in the next moment he wished he might escape the man's watchful eye altogether. If he took a great deal of time exploring the island, perhaps he need not venture out onto the marsh at all, or anywhere near the river!

At the foot of the hill the road leveled out along the point and continued over the Witches' Bridge and on through the marsh. At his right the orchard sloped down to the neat hay beds in the east. But on the other side, the wild West Marsh lay hidden behind a rise dark with pine.

Dan looked away, then back again. Had his eyes tricked him, or had he seen a house in the thicket? Curious, he left the road and climbed the knoll. With growing pleasure he followed a path through the pines, pungent and sweet in the rare rays of sunshine.

Directly ahead stood a tiny building with a steeply pitched roof. He approached, delighted. It was built of stone with a nail-studded door and narrow, arched windows set deep in mortar. It was a hushed, enchanted place out of a fairy tale, a place waiting to be awakened. The door was not locked. It moved inward with a low cry of rusted hinges.

The boy looked curiously around him. He stood in a single room, long and narrow like the nave of a small church, with three arched windows at either side. It was empty, silent. Slowly, the dust sifted downward through the beams of sunlight.

In that moment, with a sense of horror, Dan knew where he stood. This was the chapel, and it was near this place that old Daniel Pride had been found!

He turned on his heel and ran, ran—out of the chapel and down the path and back into the sunshine. There he checked himself, panting. Supposing Billy Ben were watching! Shame began to replace his panic. What had he run from? There had been nothing at all in the chapel. He was a coward and Billy Ben knew him for what he was. Worthless. And a coward.

The sky arched high and blue above the island. A blackbird, red-chevroned, flashed through the sunshine and whistled from a bush. Slowly, Dan's heart stopped pounding in his throat.

He made a swift decision. Without knowing that he did so, he glanced defiantly toward the house. He would explore, all right. He would walk calmly down the point road, and along the East Marsh through the orchard, and then to the Gut. He would show Billy Ben!

CHAPTER FIVE

The Black Dog

~~~~~~

BRAVELY enough, Dan started down the point road, whistling a tune. With each step the island, solid and safe, fell behind. The salt marsh gradually became the whole world, half land, half sea, wide and bright and windswept, and threatening.

Dan's whistle turned plaintive, like an uneasy wind. When he realized that the tune was "Danny Boy", he fell silent. The wide brown eyes of Billy Ben seemed to be at his back like a silent hand thrusting him on. On he went, to the end of the point.

Here Dan saw the gravestone. He stopped in dismay. It stood at the end of the road just short of the causeway that led to the bridge. Then he saw that this was not a grave marker, but rather a milestone. The number 37 was carved in primitive numerals above a weathered B. Boston, 37 miles. Dan looked with new interest at the narrow dirt road, once the ancient highway of the Puritans, now forgotten by the busy world.

At the head of the stone was a curious mark: a crude triangle with a smaller triangle carved inside it. Dan ran his finger wonderingly over the symbol. Three sides. The number three again, like the windows in the chapel, like the arches in the bridge beyond. Dan thought of the threes which he had met in his reading: the three fates, the mystic three of superstition. He stirred uneasily. His blistered hand throbbed under the swimming trunks which he carried. Remembering Billy Ben, he left the point road and turned east, following the field at the marsh's edge, heading slowly toward the Gut.

Gradually he became aware of a change in the salt marsh beside him. The ditches lay clean-cut and open to the river. The tide flowed through them fresh from the sea, and the grass along their borders was a brighter green than in the West Marsh.

But then Dan's spirits fell. There was no causeway leading to the Gut! The "new road" to York, built after the witch trials, lay a good mile east of the bend. To reach the Gut, then, one must walk over the marsh!

Slowly Dan followed the edge of the orchard until he was opposite the bend. Then with fast-beating pulse, he stepped out onto the marsh. His first reaction was terror, for with each step the marsh seemed to quake. But presently he saw that the turf would indeed support his weight.

Cautiously he struck out, walking parallel to a waterway. Here were no puddles of stagnant water, no salt ponds. His passage was muffled by the deep mat of grasses, but it seemed secure. Here in the East Marsh, apparently, was safety, as well as a growing harvest. With new confidence Dan shortened the distance between himself and the Gut. The tide, he thought, must be running out. From the level of the marsh, he could not see the river at all. Only a winding line of dark green marked its course.

Dan stopped for breath and glanced around to measure the distance he had covered. Already Pride's Island was a hazy half-mile or so away. Then his whole body went rigid. A few yards behind him hunched a black and brutal form, its head thrust forward as if to spring, its yellow eyes baleful and cunning.

Dan whirled and ran headlong for the river, heedless of ditch and hummock. He had no clear idea of what he would do when he reached the water. He knew only that he must outrun the monster on his trail.

Then without warning the river lay before him, low in its banks. Half-running, half-falling, he fought his way down through the mud to the water's edge. There he stood, gasping.

For a time there was no other sound except the running of the river. And stare as he would at the grassy horizon above him, no ugly black head appeared against the sky. There was nothing.

Dan groaned. He could not return by way of the marsh, and he dared not enter the water. Trapped, he turned to face the river, searching for an answer.

As he scanned the marsh line across the Gut, he looked directly into a pair of bright eyes. Here were the same eyes, the same crouched figure which he had seen in the thicket the night before! Dan stared, open-mouthed.

There on a ledge across the Gut sat a boy, squatting on his haunches. The boy was about his age, thin but taller,

his overgrown sandy hair spiking damply from his head.
As Dan stared, he burst into a roar of laughter.

"I'm no beauty, but I didn't know I was that bad! You
look like you just saw Frankenstein's monster."

Dan's face relaxed into a sheepish grin. "You surprised
me."

The boy chuckled. "*I* surprised *you!* I was about to
jump in, and you came chopping down the bank. You sure
are muddy," he added.

Dan looked down. From his knees to his feet, he had
never been so black in his life.

"I'll meet you on your side," said the boy.

Dan watched in admiration as the stranger cut into the
swift water in a perfect arc. A few yards down river he
reappeared, shook the water out of his face like a spaniel,
and struck out against the current. Then he stood beside
Dan, tall and dripping.

"I'm Pip," he said, thrusting out a wet hand.

"I'm Dan."

The two boys grasped hands simply and strongly, and
the smarting in Dan's blistered palm seemed to make the
gesture a pact of friendship.

"Might as well swim in those and wash 'em off," said
Pip, pointing to Dan's pants. "Then you won't get chewed
out when you get home," he added cheerfully.

Dan hesitated.

"You're going in, aren't you?" asked the boy in surprise.

Dan tried not to look at the rippling dark water.
"Absolutely," he said firmly. He stooped to untie his
sneakers.

"You talk funny," grinned Pip.

Dan straightened up. "Possibly because I've lived in

England for some time." He waited, his dark eyes somber. Now his new friend would put two and two together and understand that here was a Pride, not welcome in York.

Something flickered in the boy's bright eyes, but they remained clear and steady on his own. "Welcome home, Dan Pride."

Dan let out his breath. For a moment the two took each other's measure. Then, satisfied, Pip wheeled. "Come on. I'll beat you to the other side."

There was not time to be afraid. Suddenly Dan was deep in the water, the current cold against his body. He aimed for the opposite back and fought the river harder than he needed to, for his feet touched ground a little above the ledge. He had crossed the Gut! He scrambled up the path behind Pip.

"Not used to swimming, huh?" Pip was simply stating a fact.

Dan shook his head.

The blond boy flopped onto his stomach in the sun and waited for Dan to catch his breath. He was wearing a ragged pair of trunks and Dan recalled the shacks which dotted the road to York. Here, thought Dan suddenly, was his chance to ask about the local feud. He started to speak, but then changed his mind. This would be like spying on his uncle. He could put such questions to Billy Ben and Mrs. Corey, for they were part of the Pride family even as their elders had been before them.

And he decided not to mention the black dog. Perhaps, for the second time, he had only imagined it.

Instead he asked cautiously, "What do you know about signal lights that flash at night around here?"

Pip rolled onto his back and whooped with glee. "You

got the message! By golly, it was a long-shot chance, but you got it!"

Dan stared, mystified.

"Look," said Pip. "I heard you were coming. Then I saw you go by last night, looking like you'd lost your last friend. Later, a light went on in the part of the old Pride house that's always dark, so I guessed that was you. I thought you could use a little welcome."

"How did you know I understand Morse Code?"

"Took a chance. I learned it in Scouts, and hoped you did. Only I couldn't remember 'h' to say 'Hello,' or 'w' to say 'Welcome.' But I got your name out okay, didn't I?"

Dan nodded gratefully. "Thanks." So it had been a human hand, and only Pip's, behind the lights in the marsh! And the sense of mystery which haunted the old house and the West Marsh? He had imagined it, just as he had imagined the black dog.

He looked curiously at Pip. "It was pouring buckets last night when I came. Yet there you were in the thick of things at the edge of the marsh. Didn't you mind getting wet?"

Pip grinned. "That's when I like it best out here. It's wild then, and kind of—exciting."

Dan drew a careful breath. "What about during a fog? And at night?"

"Uh-uh," declared Pip. "Not me." He changed the subject. "See that eel grass down there?"

Long ribbons of green streamed upward from the channel bed, flowing in the current like shining hair. Dan suppressed a shudder. He had swum through this. "Awful stuff, isn't it? Are there eels in it?"

Pip chided him. "It's remarkable stuff. It's like an underwater forest. It's food and protection for fish and eels, and crabs—all sorts of things. And when it washes up, the redwings grab it and weave it into their nests."

Dan looked at his friend with new interest. "There's certainly a great lot of grass down there," he said politely.

"Oh, eel grass isn't a grass, it's a flowering plant. But there's plenty of grass in the marsh all right." He rolled over and yanked at a slender blade nearby. Stretching it between his thumbs, he blew a piercing blast. "That's fox grass."

"Sounds like a waterfowl I heard in England once," said Dan.

Pip grinned. "Sounds like the green herons, here. I call to 'em that way. Once I even got one to answer me. Just before you came, I was watching one over there in the black grass."

"Black grass?"

Pip pointed to a small island just beyond. "See that dark cover around the edge? It grows just above the marsh floor." The boy talked on about the birds and the small animals which lived here together. He spoke of the marsh as if he were talking about his best friend.

Dan smiled. "Billy Ben loves the marsh, too."

Unexpectedly the blond boy shook his head. "To some folks that's all the marsh is—dollars and cents." Resentfully, Pip sent a rock spinning into the creek. Then his sunny nature reasserted itself. "Say," he said, "it's good you're here! We can even send messages in code sometimes. I live down the road, so I can see your windows right across the marsh and you can see mine."

Dan looked toward a tar-roofed shack in its clearing by the road. He had been right about Pip.

The boy asked suddenly. "You already out of school for the summer?"

"My school closed early," Dan explained briefly. He hoped Pip would not want to talk about the differences between their schools—and their families. His face clouded in spite of himself.

"Lucky you," said Pip warmly. He glanced at Dan, then looked away awkwardly.

"Do you think you might teach me something about swimming?" Dan asked, changing the subject.

Pip's smile flashed in his tanned face. "Sure thing! How about tomorrow?"

"Right. Same time," Dan promised.

The boy shook his head. "I have a lawn job after school, but I can come later."

"That's all right. Same place?"

Again Pip shook his head. "The swimming's okay at the Gut when the tide's right. But it'll be gucky later on."

"Gucky?"

"Like your sneakers."

They glanced at Dan's tennis shoes on the opposite bank, twice normal size in their coating of mud, and laughed together.

"There's a good place nobody goes to much," continued Pip. "See that old bridge over there? It's supposed to be haunted, but it's the best swimming around here, any tide."

"Do you go there alone?" Dan asked, surprised.

"Uh-uh, not me," Pip said. "I only go there when I can

get someone to go with me," he confessed cheerfully. "Meet me over there tomorrow around four, okay?"

"Right," said Dan breathlessly. The boy had left him no time for thought, or anxiety. It had not occurred to Pip that Dan was afraid of things, and Dan suddenly determined that Pip should not find out.

"Go ahead. I'll see you off," said his new friend.

Dan thought briefly of the animal shape crouched in the salt grass beyond. Then he thrust it out of his mind, for of course he had imagined it. He jumped into the river and made his way to the opposite shore. This time he relaxed enough to enjoy the cool water on his blistered hand. Before he expected it, he felt the soft mud oozing up between his toes. He turned to catch Pip's wave, and to see him trot carelessly across the marsh toward the York road.

Dan had made a friend! And he had dived from a ledge, and swum alone across the Gut! Perhaps life at Pride's Point would not be so bad, after all.

He rinsed his shoes in the river, and climbed up the bank over hummocks of thatch grass. Then he retraced his path, a clear and solitary line back through the fine marsh hay, back toward Pride's Island.

It was exciting and a little nerve-wracking to walk barefoot on the marsh. At each step Dan felt the sea underfoot. He heard the faint hush of water swiftly filling up his footsteps. He saw the turf shift and settle as tide-flattened grasses stirred with his passage. And where in damper tracts the new salt grass grew fine and shiny green, it was like walking on silk.

Dan sniffed the air. Not only had the marsh a substance

all its own. It had a scent—a salty fragrance, wild and elemental. Yes, there was more to this marsh than its bright solitude here under the sun, more to it than its sound and fury during wind and rain. This half sea world was not alien, after all. Men like Billy Ben could work in it for food and shelter and fodder. They could play in it, as he and Pip had played today. In its wildness they would find not only solitude and danger, but beauty as well, thought Dan, remembering the light in Pip's face as he talked about the marsh.

Dan had almost reached solid ground at Pride's Island when he saw it. He stopped, shaken to the core. Where before, the marsh had carried no track except his own, there was now a second path branching off toward the West Marsh. It was the sort of path made by a large animal—secretive, well-defined.

And in the black silt beside the ditch, Dan saw something else. He saw the sharp, water-filled print of a huge paw!

CHAPTER SIX

Uncle Julian

Dan stared covertly at his uncle, hoping he would glance up and notice him. His story about the beast in the marsh waited impatiently on the tip of his tongue. But the meal dragged on. Julian Pride remained preoccupied with some dark concern of his own, and Dan dared not break in upon his thoughts. Would all the dinners, all the evenings to come, be like this? he wondered. It was like dining with a person already dead and lost in a world of ghosts.

Mrs. Corey came in and frowned at Dan's half-finished plate. "You clean up that apple pie," she told him tartly. "One good east wind'd blow you clean away."

His uncle looked up sharply. "What's that?"

Mrs. Corey's voice became soothing, as if she were talking to a child. "I just said a good wind'd blow young Dan away, he's that skinny."

Uncle Julian gazed toward the barn where sunset flamed on the weathercock. The wind was due east. "It will come in foggy tonight," he said. His voice was quiet, but his words had a strange effect on the housekeeper. Her hand shook as she set his coffee before him, and she hurried out of the room.

Uncle Julian frowned and lighted a cigar. "Well, what did you do today, Dan?" he asked.

"I—explored a bit." Dan hesitated over his words. How should he tell about the dog in the marsh without sounding timid and silly, as he had this morning before Billy Ben?

"And how do you like Pride's Point?" His uncle glanced impatiently at the tall clock in the corner.

"It's fine, sir. Just fine," said Dan hastily. He does not really care, thought Dan. He wants to be at work in his office. The boy looked helplessly at the pie in his plate. He began to eat fast. The deadly silence fell again like a chill wall between them. It was not important to tell about the dog.

Dan glanced up to see his uncle's eyes upon him, puzzled and disturbed.

"Did you help Billy Ben?"

"Not much, I'm afraid. I don't seem to know the right things," he added with a laugh. The laugh sounded false.

"I see. What else?"

"Well, I met a boy. He lives in one of those small houses over on the mainland."

"What work did you do for Billy Ben?"

"—A bit of clipping," said Dan reluctantly.

"That is why you are holding your hand that way." His tone was sharp. "Let me see your hand, please."

Now his uncle would see how useless he was. Slowly, Dan held up his right hand, the palm raw and torn.

Something came alive and burned in the cold eyes, then died out again. Silently Uncle Julian stirred his coffee. Then he carefully laid down his spoon. "Something is troubling you. Is it your hand?"

"Oh no, sir," said Dan. "That doesn't hurt much at all."

"Do you want to tell me what is troubling you?"

The boy frowned at his plate. Which of his troubles should he share with his uncle? There might not soon be another chance. Yes, Uncle, he could say, I am troubled because I have heard and seen a black devil dog that does not exist. And because I have no other family but you, and you don't want me. I'm troubled because people think that we Prides are—queer. And because there is something dreadful here at Pride's Point that I don't understand—something that is destroying you and may hurt me, too. And I'm troubled because—I am afraid of you.

He could not, of course, say these things.

"Well?" said his uncle impatiently.

"I thought I saw a dog," Dan began desperately, "an evil-looking dog . . ."

His uncle seemed to relax. Abruptly he excused himself, and gave one shrill whistle at the door. A moment later Dan heard the irregular padding of a large animal.

"This is Caliban," said his uncle. "Sit," he ordered.

An ugly black beast crept into the room, head low and swinging. With a malignant glance toward Dan he hunched close to the wall, his misshapen backbone out of line, his hindquarters scarred and twisted. Yet at one time he must have been magnificent. The creature sank down beside his master, and the flat head came to rest on the great paws. But the gaze of the yellow eyes, steady on Dan, was as evil as in the marsh.

"Caliban won't trouble you if you leave him alone. But stay away from him. I keep him since he is devoted to me. He was badly—hurt, once. As a result he distrusts and dislikes people."

Dan glanced from dog to master. The words applied to his uncle as well as to the brooding and suspicious Caliban. No wonder the two were close.

"I expect Mrs. Corey did her usual gossiping about her superstitions." His uncle was restlessly trying to make conversation.

"I—asked her some questions," Dan said honestly.

"What questions?"

"Well, about the witches, Samuel and Elizabeth, and how the Bishop family started the persecution. And the story of Samuel's curse." Dan chuckled, sure this was a joke they could share.

His uncle stared at him in silence. The black mood was a curtain which he could raise or lower. In a moment he would retreat behind it, leaving Dan alone again.

Uneasily Dan continued, "She told me that my grandfather didn't believe in this talk, and was collecting family records to clear up the superstition."

"He talked a great deal about writing a history, I remember. But I regret to say that no such records have ever turned up—" The voice trailed away bitterly. The lids lowered over the sunken eyes.

"At least my grandfather was trying to straighten things out with the Bishops when he died!" Dan fell silent, surprised at his daring.

"You seem to know a great deal about the family troubles. Please go on." Uncle Julian's eyes were cold. But now he was looking at Dan; he had not forsaken him for that other world of his.

"Well, she told me about the Fiddler's fog that came that same night, and how they found my grandfather, later, near the Witches' Bridge."

Something frightening was stirring in his uncle's look. But Dan had gone too far to stop. "She said his briefcase was never found, even though you and my father looked everywhere for it."

His uncle's voice was dry. "True. We did search everywhere. In the West Marsh, where we found his footprints and the mark of his case. In the chapel, on the causeway. We even searched this house, every nook and cranny. We did find a combination to a safe or strong box that fits nothing at Pride's. But no briefcase."

Dan drew a careful breath. "What was in the case?"

His uncle's bloodless face colored with emotion. "The papers, of course. Papers to prove that my father bought the Bishop property exactly as he agreed to do, paying in full that night!"

Dan remembered the housekeeper's story. "And the Bishops denied it."

His uncle laughed shortly. "Naturally. Once the briefcase with the proof was lost, they swore they never saw him that night. And the town believes the Bishops!" His voice had taken on a quality so ringing that the dog Caliban growled deep in his throat.

"Prides are men of honor," continued his uncle with intensity. "Prides have always kept their word. If we had found the briefcase, we might have proven the Bishops liars and thieves for once and all. Witch-hunters! Dishonorable people!" He steadied his voice with an effort. "Look at me, Dan."

Startled, Dan saw for a moment the depth of his uncle's hatred of the Bishops.

"I want you to promise that you will have nothing to do with any member of the Bishop family. Ever."

"Yes, sir," said Dan tightly. "I promise."

Then Julian Pride sat back as if spent, and the dark curtain dropped over his face.

After a moment Dan said carefully, "Mrs. Corey thinks she knows where the briefcase is."

His uncle did not look up.

"She thinks it's at the bottom of the big salt pond out there. She says the Fiddler did it, since my grandfather didn't believe in the curse."

Without warning, Uncle Julian came again to violence. The dark eyes burned and he struck the table with such force that the dishes clattered. "Talk! Questions and answers! Superstition! That's the ruin of this family!"

Dan sat tense and wretched.

"Questions! If you have questions, you bring them to me, do you hear? *Do you hear?*"

"Yes, sir," whispered Dan.

"Mrs. Corey is a fine woman, but she is the soul of superstition—perfect for Pride's Point." He shrugged wearily. "Nothing ever changes here, you know. The house remains the same. The people stay the same: the Prides, proud; the Coreys, hard-working, superstitious. The silence stays the same . . ." He gazed with dull eyes around the room. "Even the portraits. Old Samuel there, the witch. He never changes . . ."

Dan looked. This then was not a portrait of his uncle. This was the Fiddler! The accused witch who had uttered the curse at the bridge! Dan stared, and the keen eyes stared back as if alive.

Tentatively he said, "Billy Ben told me about Samuel Pride: how he cursed them when they arrested him for witchcraft."

"Billy Ben," said his uncle wearily. "Lately he takes too much on himself. What did he tell you?"

Dan chose his words with care. "He said that people stay away from the marsh and the bridge on foggy nights, because of Samuel's curse."

"That's true," said his uncle dryly. "According to tradition, Samuel returns to the spot where he was accused, to warn of trouble. Over the years many have heard his violin, usually in a heavy fog, and always before some calamity. So they say," he added in a bitter voice, "and few miss the opportunity of saying it."

Dan thought. "But if no one went near the marsh and never heard Samuel's ghost, what then? Wouldn't troubles come anyway?"

Uncle Julian shrugged. "York has its share of actual troubles like any other town, Fiddler or not. But those who look for trouble where there is none will find it. Evil breeds evil, you know. Fear breeds fear. Hate breeds hate." His eyes had fixed on the portrait and gone dull. It seemed as if Uncle Julian had stepped into the painting of Samuel Pride and there come to life again.

Dan said more loudly than he intended, "You said if I

have questions, I am to ask you, sir— How did they execute Samuel Pride?"

His uncle studied his cigar. Then he answered. "He was pressed to death. They placed boards upon him, then piled stone on stone, until he died."

Dan stared in horror.

"Nobody has told you why?" Malice twisted the thin face.

Dan shook his head.

"They did this to Samuel because he stood mute. He refused to speak, and death by pressing was the penalty for silence. He refused to plead innocent to the charge of witchcraft because he knew they would try him and find him guilty in any case. Those found guilty, you see, were hanged. Their lands and homes were impounded—taken away from them. By remaining silent, Samuel would lose his life. But he would save Pride's Point for the Prides. For me," added his uncle dryly, "and for you."

Startled, Dan looked up at the portrait. The dark eyes gripped his, piercing and powerful. Yes. Such a man could stay silent under torment.

Dan's throat was dry and he finished his water. "But even though Samuel actually pronounced the curse, surely the rest of it—the Fiddler's fog, the violin that warns of trouble—surely that's all superstition?"

His uncle said nothing.

Thinking he agreed, Dan went on, "Then why did the Prides stop using the old road? Why are people afraid of the marsh fogs—if it's all just superstition?" Now his uncle would say there was nothing to the myth; that like old Dan, his grandfather, they must both deny such tales.

Uncle Julian rose and threw his cigar into the hearth. The beast by the wall pulled himself up to his feet. "I wish I knew," muttered the man to himself. "I wonder, sometimes, whether Prides should quit this place, never bequeath it to another Pride—" Then he looked urgently at Dan. "In any case, you are to stay out of the marsh on foggy nights. I want your word on this."

Dan's mind rocked. *His uncle believed!* In spite of what he had said about superstition, his uncle believed in the witch's curse! The floor beneath Dan's feet became suddenly like the marsh, unsure, tremulous.

His uncle repeated forcefully, "*Your word on it, Dan!*"

"Yes, sir," said Dan.

The clock in the corner whirred and struck eight; and from the landing, the case clock echoed the strokes. Uncle Julian turned at the door as if he were completing an ordinary conversation. "I work in my office evenings. I assume you have studying to attend to. Feel free to use the books in the library. As for the telephone, it should be kept for the use of my associates in the city. When you have nothing better to do, there is a television set in the small living room in the west wing."

"Thank you, sir," said Dan formally. He stood for a minute, looking after man and dog. He pitied them both—yet he feared them, too.

Through a window he could see Billy Ben down by the kitchen garden. He was whistling cheerfully, "Oh, Danny Boy, the pipes, the pipes are callin'—"

Dan brightened. He had much to tell the hired man— about Pip, and the swim across the Gut; about his meeting with Caliban; and most of all, about his uncle. Julian

Pride, intelligent and cultured, had come to believe in Samuel's ancient curse! Billy Ben would tell him more. Dan was starting outside when he had a quick memory of his uncle's voice, authoritative, passionate: *"If you have questions, you come to me with them!"* Somehow, this was an order.

Dan climbed the stairs and made his lonely way to his room. He paused at the threshhold. His room had undergone some friendly change. Then he saw on his desk a picture which had not been there before. He studied it, his pleasure mounting. It was his father as a schoolboy, his book bag over his shoulder. In the background was a neat brick building: "York Public Library".

Dan felt a quick new hope. Wasn't this picture proof, after all, of Uncle Julian's friendship for him? Happier than he had been since his arrival, Dan spent the evening working at his desk.

But later, he waited for sleep to come. Then the darkness, and something else, took over the house. Perhaps it was only the endless marsh wind prowling in at the windows. But there seemed to be a presence abroad, restless and malevolent. Half asleep, he watched his nightmare thoughts come and go: *I am an intruder. I'm useless and unwelcome here. Something wants me gone . . .*

Late in the night, the fog moved in from the sea. Dan stirred, and shivering, pulled up his comforter.

Then, without question, he heard the faint wail of a violin. "Danny Boy," thought Dan with surprise, played over and over like the wind, sadly, with variations. Or was it "Danny Boy," or any tune he knew? Dan listened, and the wind blew the drapes and flowed like chill water over his face. The music was too faint, and he was too sleepy to be certain. But he felt quick pleasure in the thought that Uncle Julian, like his grandfather, also played the violin! Surely this meant that his uncle was not yet licked by the superstition which hagrode the family. As soon as his hand healed, perhaps they might even play together! So thinking, Dan turned over and went back to sleep.

In the gray dawn the wind turned and the fog moved blindly back to sea. Now the wetlands lay dim in the half-light. With an uncanny cry, a night heron rose from the tide line and flapped slowly upstream.

From the hushed and fog-bound marsh near the bridge had come the eerie sound of music, as it had come before. And it would come again.

CHAPTER SEVEN

The Fiddler

~~~~~~

THE jeep bounced along the narrow road that led to the East Marsh. It stirred up its own hot breeze.

"What are we going to do in York?" Dan asked eagerly.

"Just errands. But later maybe, a movie—if you like movies," Billy Ben shouted over the noise of the engine.

"You bet your life I do," said Dan.

The East Marsh lay ahead of them, shimmering in the heat of early afternoon. They started down the new road that cut straight across toward York.

Dan thought gratefully of Billy Ben's sudden invitation to go to York, for the morning had gone badly enough. After breakfast he had mastered the lawn mower, and Billy Ben had given him the task of finishing the side lawn by noon. But it had grown hot and humid, and the marsh rocked with the heat. At lunchtime he was still a long way from the end.

It had not helped to have to wear the oversized work gloves which Billy Ben handed him. "Your uncle's orders.

I guess he wants you babied," the hired man told him, trying to hide his own embarrassment. Dan reddened at the memory. Uncle Julian plainly did not care a button for Dan's pride. Therefore, Dan reasoned, he cared nothing for his nephew.

Yet difficult and morose though his uncle was, he had just shown Dan a special kindness. Or had he? With a sense of disloyalty, Dan had asked, "Billy Ben, do you know whether Uncle Julian left a picture of my father in my room?"

Billy Ben laughed shortly. "Mrs. Corey, more likely. Your uncle's got ghosts enough in his head as it is."

Disappointed, Dan had turned away.

But now, as Pride's Point fell far behind them, his spirits rose. Thankful for Billy Ben's friendship, Dan told him about meeting the boy from the shack, and about their swim at the Gut.

Billy Ben was a good listener, and Dan felt companionship grow swiftly between them.

"You were right," he said carelessly, "the water is rather fast there at the Gut."

"Weren't scared a bit, huh?" asked Billy Ben.

"There's nothing to it, really," said Dan, not meeting his eye. "But I did get a scare coming back," he added honestly. "I saw a huge footprint in the marsh."

Billy Ben glanced sharply at him.

"Do you remember telling me about the black dog they used to think haunted the marsh?"

Billy Ben nodded.

"Well, I admit I thought of that. Actually, of course, it was only that ugly dog of my uncle's. Caliban." Dan laughed.

Billy Ben did not laugh. The silence grew long and somehow chill.

Puzzled, Dan cast about for something else to say. "I got another surprise last night, too. I had no idea my uncle played the violin, until I heard him—"

Billy Ben braked the jeep to a stop. "Until you *what?*"

"Until I heard him playing last night—" Dan's voice sounded thin and lost. Even as he repeated himself, Billy Ben's face closed and told him the truth. *It was not his Uncle Julian whom Dan had heard in the night.* Who, then?

Billy Ben shook his great head. "Your uncle hasn't any fiddle. He wouldn't play it if he did." Then he added in wonder, "The fog came in last night, blessed if it didn't." He started up the jeep again.

"Maybe I dreamed it," whispered Dan. "Maybe I dreamed it," he shouted over the motor.

Billy Ben shrugged.

Dan's eyes blazed with sudden anger. "I don't believe it!" he cried. "How could a dead man, even a witch, play a violin?"

"You're doing all the talking," said Billy Ben softly.

"I'm sorry," Dan muttered. Then he added stubbornly, "But I did hear a violin."

Billy Ben looked very patient. "Okay, you heard one. Only there isn't a fiddle anywhere at Pride's. Just yours."

Dan glanced at his right hand, still too raw and stiff to hold a bow. Then he remembered something. "My grandfather's! Somebody must have been using his—"

Billy Ben shook his head. "Your granddaddy gave it away, just before he—died."

Defeated, Dan stared out at the marsh and the long

causeway fell behind them. Some dreadful thing always happened whenever the Fiddler was heard. Disaster. It might happen to him, or to anybody at all. It might happen in York or at Pride's Point. And there was nothing he or anybody else could do to stop it!

In heavy silence they turned onto the road to York. Finally, in a bleak effort to draw out Billy Ben, Dan said, "Tell me about the dog, Caliban, please."

Billy Ben snorted. "That critter isn't a dog. That devil's half nightmare, half werewolf."

"Is he really vicious?"

"He tried to kill me once," said Billy Ben simply.

Dan stared for a shocked moment. "I don't see why you stay on at Pride's!" he cried. "Mrs. Corey even says you do more than you're paid to do!"

Sudden laughter exploded from Billy Ben. "Want to know why I stick around, Danny Boy? Because old Billy Ben's a loyal Corey like his daddy before him, that's why. Anyway, there's no future in the shipyard."

Dan laughed with him, wondering what future there was in working for his ill-tempered uncle. But Billy Ben was his friend again.

They had reached town. The masts rose tall above the long buildings on the waterfront. This must be the property which his grandfather had planned to buy—and on the night when the Fiddler was last heard!

"May we see the shipyard?" Dan asked on an impulse.

"Sure," said Billy Ben. "Just don't expect the velvet carpet to be rolled out. Prides aren't too popular in York, you know."

Dan nodded. With Billy Ben along, everything would be all right. They rolled over the blistering tar to a stop.

The hot air was filled with the smell of parked cars, new wood and cordage, fresh paint, machine oil, fish and old bait, and everywhere the salt smell of the tide. Dan's senses stirred with excitement. Beyond the narrow harbor stretched the sea, gleaming like metal.

"There's the schooner they're building. Let's have a look." Billy Ben led the way past boat cradles and bright winches. The vessel rose high above the rails that led downward to the sparkling water. Her name, *Three Sisters*, had been freshly gilded at the swell of the bow. They took a short cut through a ramshackle warehouse and climbed a steep ramp onto the schooner.

"Billy Ben, boy!" came a friendly roar. Curiously, the man's manner changed. He became rougher, more blustering, as he joked with the men working on deck.

For the time being, Dan was ignored. Left alone, he explored the schooner with mounting enthusiasm. But as he rejoined the group on deck, they fell silent. Self-conscious, Dan glanced at Billy Ben.

But Billy Ben, troubled, looked away. "Tell 'em what you heard last night, Danny Boy. Must have been about the time the fog came in."

Dan stared at Billy Ben, unbelievingly. *No!* he cried in silence. *They hate me already, since I'm a Pride. If I tell them about hearing the Fiddler, the talk will start again, just as Mrs. Corey said it would.*

"Come on," urged Billy Ben impatiently. "Tell 'em, Danny Boy."

Defeated, Dan looked at the men. "I thought I heard a violin during the night."

The faces before him gazed back without expression. Now Dan knew how Samuel Pride's accusers had looked at him on the bridge. What had his uncle said so bitterly? "Those who look for trouble will find it. Evil breeds evil. Fear breeds fear. Hate breeds hate."

One of the men spoke up. He sounded puzzled. "You sure you weren't playing that fiddle yourself, Boy? For a joke, maybe?"

Swiftly Billy Ben reached out and turned Dan's hand palm up. "No sirree," he declared stoutly. "Not with this hand."

The silence grew heavy, as cold as ice.

Billy Ben said quietly, "You better go find that movie, Danny Boy. I'll be along."

Dan walked stiffly past Billy Ben, whom he had some-how failed, and on past the men, and off the schooner. He felt their eyes following him into the dusk of the ware-house. He walked on until he came to the square, with the Union soldier leaning forever on his granite gun. Directly opposite the square was the library. Dan had a nostalgic vision of his father standing on these very steps, young and smiling.

At that moment Pip himself came out with an armload of books. A cap which had seen many washings was pulled low over his shaggy head.

But no look of recognition crossed Pip's face.

"Hello!" called Dan.

Pip glanced back at the small group of boys coming down the steps behind him. Then without a word, he walked past Dan and on through the square.

Dan's face turned scarlet. He pretended to read the in-scription on the monument, his thoughts heavy. In the marshland Pip was his friend. But here in York it was a different matter.

The words engraved on the monument began to swim before his eyes: *In Memory Of The Soldiers And Sailors Of 1861–1865. One Family. One Flag.* Then followed the names. Bishops and Coreys, too, had fought in that distant war between the states. And Prides. Captain Joseph Pride had fallen at Cemetery Ridge.

Dan's chin came up. Proud men, leaders, the Prides had been. If they had not had the town's affection, at least they must often have had its esteem. Yet now it seemed that everyone in York felt free to scorn them.

Confused and miserable, Dan started walking. He felt that he could not get out of town fast enough. Billy Ben would understand. Besides, Dan had given him trouble enough for one day. The boy walked on down Main Street and away from York, blindly moving upriver.

It was intensely hot. As he started across the East Marsh, the sun beat down on his head like a punishment. But each step put his enemies farther behind him. Pride's Island, shimmering in the heat, became a stronghold, and the marsh a great moat against the foe.

Beyond Billy Ben's gardens, he turned off the road and slipped into the barn through a door at the back. Here it was vast and dim and cool. Here were stalls, still sweet with the smell of hay long since swept away. Dan sat wearily on a bench.

He would make plans to leave Pride's Point. He was not wanted here, either by his uncle or the people at Pride's, or by the town. Even his new friend Pip had rejected him.

There was no reason now to fight for a foothold in this friendless place.

At first Dan was only distantly aware of the animal sounds behind him. Then the sounds moved stealthily closer, and stopped. Suddenly fearful, Dan knew that the killer dog Caliban stood behind him. He did not stir, did not breathe.

For an endless minute, nothing. Then, slowly, Dan turned. The great beast stood motionless, his head lowered. Billy Ben's voice seemed to fill the barn: *"He tried to kill me once."* But the yellow eyes fixed on Dan were neither cunning nor evil. Instead they were watchful, as if the dog were waiting for something—a blow, perhaps, or for Dan to take flight. Dan did neither.

With a low growl, the dog sank down and rested his massive head on his paws. It came to Dan that they were both outcasts, each lonely, each suspicious of the other. Somehow he felt less alone, and the pain inside him shrank to a size that he could bear.

Hoarsely Dan tried the dog's name. "Caliban." Defensive, the beast pulled himself up to a half-crouch. He might yet attack. The two eyed each other, and did nothing, and the minutes inched on. Gradually Dan faced the fact that he could not stay here at bay indefinitely.

He forced himself to rise and turn. Slowly, he walked toward the house. Only when he reached the great door did he look back.

Caliban stood directly behind him like an ugly statue. Then he lowered his head and limped swiftly back to the barn, as if he hoped not to be seen.

Dan, with the same furtive haste, fled alone to his room.

CHAPTER EIGHT

A Swim from the Bridge

~~~~~~

DURING the endless afternoon, Dan's room was a refuge. Like a desperate animal he crouched at the window, aware of the stillness of the house, the ticking of the clock. And always the bridge like a grim mark upon them all, rocking in the heat, forever separating the Prides from the Bishops.

In a few minutes Pip would be at the bridge. But Dan would not be there to meet him. And tonight, he decided, he would talk with his uncle and ask if, when fall came, he could return to Governor.

His decision made, Dan gazed into the hot afternoon. His head ached with the heat. Then a helpless fury began to rise against his bad luck at hearing the music he knew he had heard. The fury spread to include Pip. What right did Pip have to snub him? Dan would demand to know! Swiftly, before he should decide against it he changed into his trunks, seized a towel, and charged down the point road.

The blond boy was even then crossing the bridge from Oak Island. He waved cheerfully, quite as if nothing at all had happened in York. But once beside him, Pip said with concern, "You look beat, Dan. It's the heat."

Dan said nothing.

"Let's go in before Gilly gets here! Come on, we can talk down on the landing." Pip crouched on the low wall that rimmed the bridge, then dived neatly into the center of the stream.

Impatiently Dan waited for Pip to come up. How could the boy act so friendly after the insult in York? And who was Gilly? Dan gripped the stone rail, unconsciously holding his breath.

The seconds passed. Bright and placid under the sun, the river wound idly away through the marsh. In sudden alarm Dan sprang to the opposite side of the bridge. But there was no sign of Pip, nor was there any sort of landing below.

Dan leaned over the parapet as far as he dared. Directly beneath, he saw his own anxious image, blurred and mobile in the gloomy water. At either side of the arch rose the dripping stonework. But there was nothing else.

"Pip!" Dan's voice was tense and high-pitched. The echo came back from under the bridge like a hollow mockery.

Dan kicked off his sneakers and put one foot over the rail. Then he hesitated, his heart pounding shamefully. Below ran the river, swift and black. How can I help Pip if I jump? he asked himself. It will be all I can do to help myself! Then a bitter self-loathing came over him. Dan tensed himself to leap, when he heard swift footsteps.

He stared in horror. For a figure was coming toward him, dark against the evil glint of Bella, the salt pond— and the figure was Pip's. Yet Pip was bone dry. His dry hair was blowing back from his forehead. His dry shirt was rippling in a sudden breeze. For a terrible instant it seemed that Pip had drowned and had now, somehow, risen from the salt pond. Suddenly all the evil stories of this place came true. The Witches' Bridge had added another tragedy to its list . . .

"Hi," said the image of Pip quite normally. "So you're the boy outside the library! You were waiting for someone behind me."

Dan stared dumbly.

Laughing, the image thrust out a hand. "I'm Gilly, Pip's twin sister. Didn't he even tell you I was coming?"

Twin sister. Then Dan's mind went careening back to Pip. "Pip dived off the bridge and hasn't come up yet!" he cried. "Do you understand? He's still down there!"

Alarm came and went again in the girl's bright eyes. "Did you look down by the bend?" Swiftly she drew Dan toward the Oak Island end of the bridge, and pointed downstream. "See? He's just ridden the current down to the landing."

From here Dan could see a granite ledge that circled the bend of the river like an arm. There lay Pip, raptly watching something.

"Look," breathed Gilly. "A great blue heron!"

The magnificent bird stood motionless in the marsh. Even as they watched, it rose into the air and flapped majestically away over their heads. Eyes shining, Dan watched it out of sight.

Gilly said, "Pip knows all about them, where they nest and everything. He carves models of all the marsh birds—good ones, too." She broke off and shouted her brother's name.

The figure on the ledge stirred itself, then leaped into the river. Presently Pip pulled himself dripping over the rail. "Couldn't you let me lay and watch him, Gilly," the boy complained cheerfully, "instead of scaring him off?"

"Lie," Gilly corrected. "And I didn't scare him, Pip Cole. He got tired of being stared at and just took off, and you know it."

Dan was looking from the girl to her twin brother, then back again. Gilly was smaller, about Dan's own height, he thought, with girlish features and build. But there the difference ended. Bright blue eyes, bright hair, tanned face, warm smile—all exactly the same as Pip's. No wonder he had taken Gilly for her twin this afternoon in York!

Gilly grinned. "You must have got good and mad at Pip over in town today."

Dan smiled back. "I'm afraid so."

"Mad at me?" Pip was honestly bewildered. "What for?"

"He thought I was you," said Gilly. "And I didn't answer because I thought he was speaking to someone else."

Pip sighed. "This happens all the time," he told Dan. "Be glad you don't have a twin sister getting you all fouled up."

Gilly sniffed. "You better be glad I'm around to keep fishing you out of trouble!" She slipped off her shirt, eagerly eyeing the water.

"Come on! So-deep!" cried Pip.

Dan hesitated.

"There's nothing to it," said Gilly kindly. "Just hold your breath and jump, and you'll fetch up down on the landing."

"Get between us," Pip added, understanding. "Then Gilly won't duck me."

Dan stood on the stone rail between the twins. Could it be possible that only minutes ago he had stared with terror at this same sparkling water? And not long since had thought of Pip with fury and a sense of deep injury?

"One, two, three, so-deep!" shouted Pip, as they took a deep breath. They splashed together into the river.

The cool force of the current bore Dan onward with a sense of tremendous speed. He felt an instant of panic, a few moments of exhilaration, and then he came against the hard warmth of the ledge.

Pip and Gilly made room for him beside them. "Want to do it again?"

Pleasure leaped high in Dan's throat. "Again and again!" he laughed, shaking the water out of his face. In the excitement of riding the current with his new friends, he forgot the black scene at the shipyard. Soon he even began to feel at home in the swift water.

"What happens if you miss the landing on the way down?" he asked as they sat in the sun, later on, to rest.

"Nothing," said Pip. "Below these narrows the river broadens out and you could climb out anywhere you wanted to. Then beyond the Gut lots of creeks flow into the river, so many I've never even explored them all. I've followed a raft of 'em, though, in our punt."

Dan had a quick vision of the decrepit boats pulled up in front of the shacks across the marsh.

"I hate that punt," said Gilly in disgust. "She skids out from under you when you're not looking."

"You just don't know how to handle her," chuckled her brother.

"I wish we could buy a decent boat. Then we could ride the river down through the marsh as far as we liked—" she said wistfully.

Pip nodded. "If the tide was going out, I bet we could get to the harbor without once rowing. Except first we'd fetch up on that point at Lamie's Island."

"Oh, no," said Gilly. "Not Lamie's!"

"What's wrong with Lamie's Island?" asked Dan, trying to recall Billy Ben's words.

"Lamie," said Gilly. "He's—queer."

"Lamie's a hermit," Pip added practically. "He lives on an island in the East Marsh in a driftwood shack, and he comes to town now and then in an old lobster boat. He's older than the hills and crazy as a loon."

Dan frowned. Then Billy Ben was right. Here was something else to fear.

"He's okay if you leave him alone," said Pip.

Like Caliban, thought Dan with dismay.

"He's supposed to be dangerous," said Gilly. "But if we had a boat we could just float by and get a look at him."

"We do have a boat," Dan said reluctantly. "There's a skiff stored in the barn. Billy Ben said I might have it. It needs work, though—"

"Billy Ben!" Gilly sniffed. She widened her eyes and grinned broadly in an excellent imitation of Julian Pride's yard man. "Well, if it isn't Dan Pride himself! There's no one I'd rather see right here at Pride's, no sirree!"

"Gilly!" Pip said warningly. "We'll help with the skiff, Dan. Can you get her down here?"

"Come along up now," Dan urged. "If Billy Ben is back, I'm sure he'll help bring it down, and find us a mooring place as well."

Gilly glanced at her brother in alarm, and Pip said hastily, "No, thanks. We've got to get going pretty quick."

"Tomorrow then," urged Dan.

But Pip shook his head firmly. "If you can get her down here, we'll help fix her up. We'll even bring some stuff to fix her up with," he added, as if to make up for his unwillingness to go beyond the causeway.

Then Dan understood. The twins would feel uncomfortable in the big old house at Pride's Point.

"All right," he agreed. "Tomorrow it is."

That settled it. The skiff was as good as launched, and they swam back to the bridge for a final dive.

This time Dan jumped last and came up directly underneath the bridge. On an impulse he decided to swim upstream and take a quick look at the causeway from the water. Perhaps he himself could find a place to moor the skiff.

It was another world here under the bridge, sunless and dank, and filled with the noise of the river. Half swimming, half pushing against the slippery arch, Dan made his way against the current and around the bridge. Here he treaded water and stared around him.

He was in a backwater, a small pool, quiet and apart from the race of the river. Weeds twined upward from the bottom like long dark fingers reaching for his legs, hiding whatever lay beneath. The earlier panic began to rise. Dan fought it down, kicking and clawing his way along the slimy face of the causeway wall.

Uneasy though he was, he could see that his Puritan forefathers had built strong and true. For the most part the stones were still solid, finely fitted and firmly mortared. Only in one place there had been a cave-in at the tide level. And just above high water, one flat rock the size of a mill wheel thrust out from the rubble.

Dan swam closer. The crumbled foundation beneath was reinforced by years of silt from the river. And the rock itself, jutting out just below the causeway level, could be reached from the road. They could use the rock as a float, launching the skiff into the quiet backwater at high tide! At other tides they could lower and raise it easily enough along the slippery bank. Elated, Dan knew he had found his mooring place.

Then he saw something else. Directly beneath the flat rock was a stone, arched and smooth like a milestone, with a faint mark at its top that set his scalp prickling. The double triangle! It was crudely carved, like its twin on the ancient milestone on the point road below the chapel. But this figure was worn almost smooth by the age-old rush of water.

Dan stared, his thoughts racing. Then he struck out into the current and let the swift river carry him under the bridge and on down to the landing.

Pip helped him up, strangely silent.

"Where've you been?" cried Gilly angrily.

Then Pip stormed in high dudgeon, "Don't you know enough to keep someone with you when you swim?"

Not at all anxious about himself, Dan burst out laughing. "Exactly what you put me through, Pip, a while ago."

A sheepish grin spread over Pip's face, and Gilly raised her eyes in despair. "Now I've got myself two idiots to look after!"

"Wait till you hear what I found!" said Dan. He told them about the flat rock in the causeway wall, and began to describe the curious mark in the stone beneath it.

But Pip and Gilly were more interested in a mooring. "Let's have a look at the flat rock," said Pip, and he took a running dive into the river.

This time, with the twins treading water beside him, Dan forgot his first terror of the pool. They sized up the mooring rock and its easy approach from the river and from the road above.

"Beautiful!" Gilly exulted.

Pip nodded. But he also took in the dark backwater with its writhing eel grass and the river skirring by. Then he punched Dan's shoulder as if he admired something else even more than the mooring rock. For the first time in his life, Dan tasted the sweetness of the pride which one friend feels for another.

To hide his feelings he pointed to the mark in the arched stone beneath the mooring rock. "You see? The double triangle. Exactly like the one in the milestone on the point road. Only no numerals to show distance, you see. Just this strange figure at the top."

Pip shrugged cheerfully, and the twins spashed their way up onto the mooring rock.

Gilly teased, "I like the way you say 'figger'. It makes you sound like Sherlock Holmes."

Disappointed, Dan sat down between them. Neither Pip nor Gilly was interested in the mystery of his double triangle.

But he knew something that would get a rise out of them. "Let's see what you make of this, then." Swiftly, as if he were unloading a burden, he said, "I heard a violin last night—faint and far off, but it was a violin all right. I heard it late in the night, I think—and Billy Ben said the fog was in."

He waited. *They look guilty,* he thought suddenly, *as if this reminds them of something bad, something important.*

Finally Pip said, "We already heard."

Dan studied his friend's closed face with a heavy heart. Some secret stood between him and the twins. Did they believe that he, Dan Pride, would in some uncanny way bring disaster?

Gilly blurted, "I think it's terrible Dan had to be the one to hear the Fiddler. You know what some people will say now!"

Pip nodded, disgusted. "That trouble's coming. What a darn-fool idea. But they'll say it. Or Billy Ben will."

Dan breathed more easily. The twins, at least, did not believe that he, like Samuel Pride, was some agent of the devil.

"Poor Mr. Pride," said Gilly unexpectedly. "He's scary, but I feel sorry for him. All those stories about the Prides. They say he hates those stories like poison."

"It's worse than that," Dan said slowly. "I think he's coming to believe in them."

"Well, you haven't helped any," said Gilly honestly. "This business of yours about hearing the Fiddler could really send him off his rocker!"

Her brother turned on her. "Gilly, for Pete's sake!"

Gilly turned a faint pink. "I'm sorry, Dan. I forgot for a minute he's your uncle. But I guess you know he's sort of—queer. Especially about those old stories."

"All that cussed foolishness just goes on forever," Pip said, "getting bigger and making more trouble between folks."

"That's what Mother says," nodded Gilly.

"You don't believe the stories, then?" Dan asked hopefully.

Pip said, "We've always heard them around town, so I guess we've always believed them. Anyway, a lot of funny things have happened."

"Such as what?" Dan asked.

"Well, of course the witch Samuel Pride started the whole thing with that curse of his, right here on the bridge. It was night, and a thick of fog, both times they came for the witches. And whenever trouble has come since then, lots of folks have sworn they heard the Fiddler warn of it, out in the fog." Pip hesitated. "You must know what happened to your grandfather, right here in the West Marsh. Night again, Fog again. And they say they heard the Fiddler just before it happened."

Dan was silent. The pool was all in shadow now, and the marsh wind flicked its surface.

"Things like that are queer enough, even if you do believe in a curse," Pip added. "But they don't make *any* sense if you don't."

"And you, Gilly?" asked Dan.

Gilly whispered thoughtfully.

"*'Out of the night, and the fog, and the marsh, these three,*

Doom shall come for thee.'

I don't know. Sometimes I just laugh at things like that. But in a way," she mused, "I believe them."

The sun had moved behind Oak Island and the arched shadow of the bridge fell across the three on the mooring rock. They walked, shivering, back along the causeway. As they toweled themselves dry, an automobile moved across the East Marsh. The low sun flashed from its windows.

Pip said softly, "He's coming."

In the next instant, the twins were off across the bridge.

Dan looked anxiously after them. Were they running away from Julian Pride because they thought him "queer"? Perhaps, like old Lamie, "as crazy as a loon"? A strange loyalty to the uncle who cared nothing for him kept Dan silent, though his spirits fell. Perhaps the twins did not mean to come back.

Then Pip called over his shoulder, "See you tomorrow!"

Gilly waved cheerfully. And the thicket on Oak Island hid the two from sight.

For a long moment Dan gazed after them across the bridge. The twilight began to set the marsh afire and let loose the shadows. Quickly he scooped up his towel and headed for the house, putting behind him the bridge, and the causeway, and the silent chapel hidden on the point.

CHAPTER NINE

The Jinx

~~~~~~

THE uneasy thought that Julian Pride was considered a sort of devil was still with Dan at dinner that evening.

His uncle ate slowly, from long and lonely habit. It was a simple matter then, for Dan to study the face before him. Brooding and sunken it was, and darkly handsome. And it was a haughty face, somehow frightening. But it was not the face of a devil. His uncle's face held misery, but not evil.

Suddenly Dan realized that Uncle Julian, home late from Boston, could not know of the violin in the night. Should he himself be the one to tell the news? Dan cast about for an easier topic to break the silence between them.

He began hopefully, "Someone left a picture of my father in my room."

Slowly his uncle returned from that land of the mind where he often wandered alone. "You should thank Mrs. Corey for that. Consider it yours, of course," he added.

Another silence, and Dan tried again. "I've a new friend, you know. We went swimming today, he and his sister and I."

The low voice sharpened. "Where do these children live?"

Dan's chin came up and for an instant the same proud spark flickered in both pairs of eyes. "In a shack across the marsh."

The heavy lids dropped. The curtain of silence fell again. His uncle was not interested in anything Dan did, so long as he stayed away from the marsh at night—and the Bishops. Very well then. It was time for Uncle Julian to sit up and take notice.

Dan threw caution to the winds. "Last night, very late, I heard a violin. The fog had come in, so I expect I heard the Fiddler."

The room seemed to stop breathing.

"Soon, I suppose, if there is a curse, something dreadful will happen."

Carefully, Mrs. Corey set down the coffeepot. Uncle Julian laid down his fork. Dan's heart began to pound in his throat.

"At least that's what people will say, won't they? And possibly they'll wonder if I had something to do with it, like Samuel the witch—" Dan broke off, suddenly frightened at his uncle's look.

Nobody moved. The great clock in the corner gave its warning whir, then struck the hour. Eight o'clock.

"Excuse me," said Uncle Julian quietly. He rose and left the room. He seemed to make a special effort to hold his tall figure erect, but he could do nothing about the whiteness of his face.

Mrs. Corey came to life. "Now see what you've done, Dan Pride! His own kith and kin!"

Dan stared, bewildered.

Her tongue raced on, stumbling with emotion. "All his life when anything turrible does happen in this town, it gets laid at his door, just like Prides was to blame! It's getting so the poor man's wondering if the Prides really do bring trouble, and whether the Fiddler does come and warn of it, and whether next time, or the next, some turrible thing'll happen again to the Prides themselves!"

Dan felt as cold as ice.

"And you've got no call to make things worse'n they are already. The poor man didn't have to take you in, you know. In the beginning, he didn't even want to!"

Dan looked up. Did Mrs. Corey mean that lately—?

"It's turrible hard for him to be friends with folks. He's out of the habit. But in case you want to know, he was up to your room just yesterday, making sure 'twas cozy. He gave me a picture of your pa to put up, so as you'd feel to home. And if I was you, Dan Pride, I'd feel some ashamed of myself!" Mrs. Corey trotted out of the dining room and firmly closed the door.

The clock ticked on. Miserably, Dan grew aware of the mistake he had made. His uncle had not hated him. Rather, he had needed Dan, just as Dan himself needed Uncle Julian.

Sick with self-reproach, he gazed at the portrait of Samuel. The splendid dark eyes drew Dan's like a lodestone. A strange excitement gripped the boy, for the eyes seemed to hold his. The ticking of the old clock filled the room, faded. For one clear, unnatural moment, it seemed to Dan that Samuel, with his piercing eyes, was all but shouting a message. Then Dan's vision shifted. The eyes were only black painted eyes on an ancient canvas.

Unsteadily Dan rose and went to his room. But the self-reproach stayed with him all that restless night.

And in the morning it haunted him like a bad dream that does not end when the night is over. Remorseful, he yanked at the weeds in the kitchen garden. I was baiting Uncle Julian for not being friends, he thought, when all along he was trying. All along his uncle had felt affection and had not known how to show it, and in one boorish move Dan had destroyed it!

Now, from the depths of his being, Dan was sorry. And he had to find a way to prove it. At least, he told himself thankfully, I didn't ask about leaving Pride's in the fall. After last night, his uncle might give his permission all too readily.

So passionately did Dan work that Billy Ben, arriving suddenly from the big garden, was moved to a round compliment. Then he added soberly, "Look, Dan, I felt like the devil yesterday when I couldn't find you. Guess you changed your mind about staying in town."

"I expect I should have waited—" Dan began, pleased with Billy Ben's concern.

"But I don't blame you for running," continued Billy Ben, "and if I were you, I'd keep out of town for a while. Folks don't feel any friendlier, now you've heard the Fiddler." He chewed on his cheek, and a little cold fear began to grow inside Dan.

"What did they say?"

'They say you're trouble, Danny Boy. A jinx, sort of."
He spoke very gently.

Dan stared at the flower bed. A jinx.

"It's crazy." Billy Ben shook his great head. "But that
foolishness about the witch's curse and all, just gets worse
instead of better."

Dan nodded. The twins had said the same thing. If only
Billy Ben himself had not mentioned that Dan had heard
the violin.

"I wish I knew what to do about it," he said desperately.

"This isn't anything new, you know. Prides aren't considered good luck." Billy Ben's voice was dry. "But you
just keep clear of trouble. Give 'em a chance to forget it.
Maybe nothing'll happen anyway."

Bleakly Dan wondered how he could keep clear of
trouble that might happen to others.

"It's a real mess, isn't it, Danny Boy?" Billy Ben stooped
to replace a loose brick in the border, but his gaze remained on Dan, pitying, all-knowing.

Reddening, Dan looked away.

Just beyond the corner of the ell was a shadow. Caliban! Pure hatred burned in the beast's eyes, and Dan felt
panic flare into his face.

Warned, Billy Ben whirled around just as the dog
moved onto them. As swift as thought, he drew back his
arm and hurled the brick. "Out!" he screamed. "Out, you
devil!" The brick missed the dog by a fraction of an inch.
Violence blazed in the yellow eyes and the dog crouched
low to spring.

But incredibly, nothing happened. In another moment Caliban turned. Slowly he moved away into the shrubs like some grotesque monster in a nightmare.

Billy Ben's face was livid. He seemed to be fighting to hide his fear and fury. Noisily he let out his breath. "Someday that dog'll kill someone!"

Dan's legs had gone weak, his palms were wet. He was remembering how the creature had trailed him to the house.

"I got to talk your uncle into letting me tie him up, days. That feller can get his exercise when the rest of us are safe in bed."

Dan recalled his uncle's loyalty to the outcast. "Will Uncle Julian allow it?"

Billy Ben shrugged. "Who wants a killer around that might hurt his own nephew? Not even Julian Pride, I hope!"

Dan bit his lip.

Billy Ben poked him cheerfully in the shoulder. "Just you keep yourself clear of trouble, Danny Boy."

He turned to leave, but Dan put out a hand to stop him. "Please, can't I help you?" If he could work side by side with Billy Ben, things might be the same as they were before he had heard the Fiddler.

Billy Ben laughed. "No sirree! You're too valuable weeding the posies."

Dan smiled wanly. After all, the drainage work was Billy Ben's special project, his own hobby. Dan asked instead about the skiff.

Now Billy Ben was all enthusiasm. "Tell you what! After lunch we'll fetch her down to the causeway. She'll

keep you out of mischief for a while, getting her ship-
shape and exploring in her. Just clear out of the marsh
before dark, that's all." He winked, as if they shared a
macabre secret. Then off down the path he went swiftly
and silently, the green of his clothing blending with the
green of the hedge. He struck up a song in a fine, full
voice, and the words came back on the morning air. "Oh,
Danny Boy, the pipes, the pipes are callin', From glen to
glen and down the mountainside—, The summer's gone
and all the roses fallin', 'Tis you, 'tis you must go, and I
must bide—."

Dan sobered, and a heaviness settled upon him. *A jinx,
Danny Boy. Just you keep clear of trouble, Danny Boy.*

Dan threw himself into his work trying to forget Billy
Ben's words; trying to forget the trouble between him and
his uncle. A fresh breeze blew from the west and the
marsh was brilliant with earth greens and sky blues. He
tackled the great back lawn, deciding for himself where to
start, and mowed long straight lines through the lush
grass. He was finding that he could be of service here at
Pride's Point, after all. Only now that he had repaid his
uncle's groping kindness with cruelty, the chores no
longer seemed important.

At one point he looked around him and saw that Pride's
was indeed beautiful. A strange, compelling love of the
place, and a new feeling of belonging, rose strongly inside
him. He had to stay! He had to prove to Uncle Julian that
he wanted to be friends!

Suddenly Dan stopped, and the motor beat heavily in
the air. There was a way to prove his loyalty! With a sense
of awe, he turned off the motor. The answer was so sim-

ple, so obvious, that the stillness shouted with it. *He would find the lost briefcase!*

Dan leaned on the mower and stared out over the marsh. If he could find the briefcase and clear Old Dan's name, then surely Uncle Julian would love him as a son. For his uncle's bitterness, Dan knew, must have started with Old Dan's death, and the slur cast on his honor by the Bishops. Finding the case would prove that his grandfather had bought and paid the Bishops for the shipyard that night. Finding the case would be proof indeed of Dan's loyalty!

Dan finished his work quickly. He was more excited than he had ever been in his life. True, Uncle Julian and the rest of the household had turned Pride's Point upside down in their search for the briefcase. But somehow, *he* must be the one to find it!

Thoughtfully Dan gazed toward the West Marsh, and thence around the island. He put away the mower, hardly aware of what he was doing. His promise to himself filled his mind: he would find the briefcase, no matter what it cost him.

No matter, even, that the old question still remained unanswered: Who or what was the Fiddler? He had certainly heard a violin at dawn. But Billy Ben had said there was no violin near Pride's, and no violinist except young Dan Pride. *It would seem then, that the Fiddler was not human.*

Then came a thought somehow even more frightening. What of his own violin hidden deep in his closet? Had someone, for dark reasons of his own, played it that night? Dan made for the house, taking the stairs three at a time.

The violin was well back in his closet where he had left it. He took it out of its case and caressed the wood, the loosened strings. Then he hid it away again like an evil thing. No one had touched it. This was the only violin at Pride's Point, and it had not been played in weeks.

Dan stared out at the bridge, silent in the peace of late morning. But there was no peace in his mind. Had he heard a violin, or not? Was he a jinx, as some people seemed to think?

That afternoon he put the question to Pip. The boy had come alone to the bridge, and they were hard at work on the skiff overturned in the grassy place by the old milestone.

"Why?" he demanded. "Why should I be the one to hear the music? Mine is the only violin around here and I certainly didn't play it, and I swear no one else did. It hasn't been touched!"

Pip sanded the hull. He looked uncomfortable.

"Pip," said Dan bluntly, "Do they think in town that— I'm a jinx?"

Pip shrugged. "I guess some folks say it's a bad sign you play the violin, like Old Dan, and then heard the Fiddler, too. It's just talk. But I wish I knew who started that foolishness."

"It's all because of who I am," said Dan bitterly. "Samuel Pride, the witch. Dan Pride, the jinx. Believe anything of the Prides!" Fury surged up in a blinding flood against the narrow-minded men of York, against the Bishops who had started it all.

Dan's voice rose. "It's the Bishops! They've hounded my

family for years with their lies. They've blamed the Prides for all the troubles York ever had. Well, no wonder my uncle is the way he is! No wonder my father left this place!"

Pip seemed to make up his mind. "Listen. There's something you better know—."

Dan interrupted bitterly. "I know quite enough, thanks. I know they'll spread rumors about my family till they finally get rid of us!" Resentful, Dan crushed his used sandpaper into a ball and hurled it into the marsh. "It's always the Bishops. They began the whole thing and they've kept it going. But here's one Pride who'll fight back." Dan stared with a hard face toward the Bishops' house on the mainland. "I only hope I never have to meet them!"

"Listen, Dan." Pip's voice sounded strained.

"I'm through listening. Now I'm going to do something. I'm going to find my grandfather's briefcase!" He paused. "You can help, if you like."

Pip remained silent, and Dan swept on. "Do you know what's in that briefcase? Proof that the Bishops are liars— thieves, perhaps."

Pip looked uncertain, his serenity gone.

"You know the story, don't you? The Bishops claim my grandfather never bought the shipyard, never even got to their house that night. Well, the Prides know better, Pip. My grandfather never would have paid that money without getting papers to prove it. Someone, one of the Bishops, or someone hired by them, followed him home to steal the briefcase and destroy the proof. But Old Dan outwitted them—only he died before he could tell the family where he hid the case."

Pip stirred, but Dan said bitterly, "Did the Bishops ever come forward and tell the truth? Did they ever turn over the property to Uncle Julian or my father? What do you think?"

"If you'd shut up and listen—" Pip began. But he sounded already beaten.

"I'm going to find those papers," Dan said tightly, "and prove that the only jinx around here is the Bishops, not me. And not Samuel Pride, or his ghost either!" A little embarrassed by his outburst, Dan added more quietly, "We'll find that case, Pip, you and I together." He reached into the tool box for a carpenter's crayon. "And just to keep it in mind, I hereby christen our skiff *Jinx*." He printed the letters on the stern. "J-I-N-X. Just to remind us of the Bishops!" Then he sat back on his heels for Pip's approval.

But Pip was shaking his head. "Why don't the Prides just forgive the Bishops, after all this time? Not keep ahold of that old grudge—"

Dan broke in, "*Forgive!*"

Silently Pip mixed the white paint with a stick, round and round.

Dan watched him, disappointed. Pip was not going to join him against the enemy after all. Dan's detective work would have to be done alone.

"So we don't agree on the Bishops," said Dan coldly. "As far as I'm concerned they're a bloody lot of witch-hunters—criminals, really. And there are facts to prove it!"

The two boys painted in chill silence. The afternoon sun still shone, and the breeze blew fresh with spruce from the northwest. Yet the brightness had gone out of the day.

Pip blurted suddenly, "You and I can't help what's happened to folks before. Most of 'em are dead anyway. So why worry about it? Let's forget it, Dan."

"You forget it," Dan said roughly. "You don't have to live with it."

The two worked on without a word. Pip finished his side of the hull and began to clean his brush on a stone. His face was so long with misery, so unlike himself, that Dan's temper began to cool.

A flock of tiny brownish birds wheeled in formation and alighted on the flats nearby, whistling and running on little yellow legs at the water's edge.

"Look there," said Dan, eager to change the subject. "What are they?"

"Mud-peeps," said Pip with relief. "The littlest of the sandpipers. They're hard to carve, they're so little. And over in the thatch," he added softly, "is a cousin of theirs, a grassbird. He's telling you his address. Listen."

The bird teetered on his perch, calling a grating *"Creek, creek."*

They laughed and the bird flew off. Everything was all right again. Dan said hesitantly, "Do you want to know something, Pip?"

Pip waited.

"You're the only real friend I've ever had, you know."

Pip grinned broadly and Dan added, "After all I've said, I certainly hope the Bishops aren't friends of yours!"

Pip thrust his brush half-cleaned into the can of turpentine. There was an odd look on his face. "I've got to go," he said abruptly. Before Dan could reply, he was swallowed up by the scrub on Oak Island.

Startled, Dan thought back over the conversation. You're the only real friend I've ever had, he had frankly told Pip Cole. Dan reddened at the thought of the sentiment he had shown. He would not make that mistake again.

He returned to his painting. Before the afternoon was out, he had finished the hull. He surveyed the skiff with pride. He had learned from Pip how to caulk and sand and paint a boat. Another afternoon with the twins' help, and the *Jinx* would be ready for the water!

CHAPTER TEN

A Fiddler's Fog

~~~~~~

INSIDE the cool old kitchen Dan poured himself a lemonade. He sat down to take a breather from his morning chores.

"You listen hard," said Mrs. Corey, "and you'll hear the foghorn all the way from the harbor." Between her eyes was that deep line that came whenever she was worried.

Puzzled, Dan looked out. The sun beat clear and hot onto the cutting garden which he had just been weeding. There was not a trace of fog lying on the river or moving up the marsh.

Then he heard it, low and faint. The steady moaning of the foghorn in a minor key, over and over again.

Mrs. Corey chopped rhubarb stalks into neat, roseate chunks. "Your uncle will be home in good season today. He gets back to the island early when it's coming a thick of fog."

Early, thought Dan gratefully. Perhaps today then he and his uncle could talk together. For last night Uncle

Julian had not returned at all for dinner. Dan had had no chance to tell him of his resolve to find the lost briefcase, to learn what places at Pride's Point had already been searched. If the fog brought his uncle home early, there might be time before dinner for the talk they must have.

But his next thought was less pleasant. "Will this be—a Fiddler's fog?" he asked.

" 'Twill be if it decides to move in," Mrs. Corey said tartly. She squinted at the weathercock on the hay barn. "Wind's coming east right now. It'll be cold and clammy by middle the afternoon. You'll see."

Fog or not, thought Dan stubbornly, by the end of the day they would have the skiff ready for the water. That is, if the twins did not let the weather keep them at home.

Mrs. Corey chatted on, rolling out her pastry. "Billy Ben's in town for cement to fix the foundation of the old chapel."

Dan nodded, remembering sharply the silent stone room, the nameless horror. "My uncle is lucky to have Billy Ben working for him."

"Prides always been lucky to have Coreys working for them," she declared. "Billy Ben's smart, too. He doesn't wait to be told things. He sees they need doing, and he does 'em. He'll get somewhere."

Dan, half listening, was eyeing the gilded weathercock on the hay barn. It pointed due east. He found himself wondering if he would again hear the Fiddler. The thought was like a cloud blotting out the sun.

"You had a look right then that put me in mind of your Uncle Julian," said Mrs. Corey. "Like you was listening for something."

Dan rose quickly. "I expect I was listening for the fog-horn."

"Real mournful. You can't get away from a foghorn."

Dan found himself listening tensely as he finished the weeding. The regular moaning seemed to fill the air. Once he heard something else—a long-drawn baying that raised the hair on the back of his neck. Just below Billy Ben's cottage he could see part of a wire runway. This, then, was where the dog Caliban was spending his days. Dan shuddered and felt a swift gratitude toward Billy Ben.

Later, on his way down to the causeway, Dan saw that Mrs. Corey was right about the weather. The fog had been moving in silently since noon. Now it hung, gray, and wet, over salt marsh and islands alike. Oak Island seemed to float between earth and sky, and the York shore was already hidden from sight. Somewhere in this vast, white world was the lost briefcase. Somehow, he must yet talk Pip and Gilly into helping him in his search—if indeed they came at all today!

Dan found himself running anxiously to the little field by the milestone. When he saw the twins already hard at work on the boat, he remembered not to show the pleasure he felt.

Pip straightened, grinning. "She's dry as a bone, Dan, fog or not. All ready for the next step."

Dan looked at his friend with relief. Whatever had troubled Pip yesterday was forgotten today.

"Next step's her name," said Gilly eagerly. "We brought some black paint and a couple of small brushes. What'll we name her, Dan?"

Dan glanced in surprise at Pip. Had he said nothing to

Gilly about Dan's hatred of the Bishops and the name that would keep that hatred before them? But Pip was measuring guide lines on the stern, his face blank, as if he had decided it was none of his business what Dan called the skiff, or why.

"I know what to name her," said Gilly suddenly. "Listen."

Dan heard a faint, regular booming, as if someone far off were driving stakes into the marsh. *Unk*-a-chunk, *unk*-a-chunk.

"That's a bittern," grinned Pip, "a marsh bird. Everyone around here calls 'em stake-drivers. I've spotted her nest down in the black-grass in the little island above the Gut. I'll show you when the skiff's finished," he promised.

"Bitterns roam the marshes, the way we'll be doing," added Gilly. "*Bittern's* a good name for the skiff."

"I've already named her, thanks," said Dan flatly. "*Jinx*."

"*Jinx*." Gilly frowned. "That name sounds like trouble, and we've had trouble enough getting Mother to let us—"

Gilly stopped. Across Pip's face had flashed that look of warning that told Dan again of the secret thing that stood between him and the twins. He thought back over Gilly's half-finished sentence. The twins were having difficulty in getting permission to come here, that was it. The Prides, and Pride's Point. One stayed away from them.

Gilly's face softened. "I'm sorry, Dan. *Jinx* is fine. Line up the letters, Pip."

His tongue carefully poised, her brother was measuring

the letters: *J, I, N, X*. He handed one of the brushes to Dan. "Here. You work on the *J* while I do this end."

The awkward moment passed. The two boys painted in contented silence while Gilly sat on the milestone and watched.

A seagull came and went in the mist. Somewhere beyond Oak Island a crow called, and called again. Dan sensed a deep peace in all this, a beauty which he had never known before he came to Pride's. Yet, just outside the warm circle of their friendship lurked something chill and menacing. Somewhere beyond this little field was the lost briefcase, the lost proof of Bishop guilt.

"How about it, Pip?" he asked, with an attempt at lightness. "Where do you think my grandfather hid that case of his? Why not hunt for it together, the three of us?"

Pip met his sister's sharp glance.

"Don't you know the story, Gilly?" said Dan. "It happened a long—"

"Gilly knows," said Pip shortly.

Gilly changed the subject, her tongue stumbling in haste. "Do you think it'll rain and ruin the paint?"

Pip shook his head. "It's not that sort of fog." He seemed relieved that they were out of some danger zone.

Gilly continued to squint upward, her eyes narrowing. "It's worse. It's coming in a Fiddler's fog, that's what. A real pea-souper."

Dan filled his brush carefully, as Pip was doing, smoothing out each previous stroke. But all his senses tensed as he waited to hear more.

"Gilly," said Pip suddenly, "how about making us a fire? That wind's getting cold and raw."

"Sure," said Gilly. She jumped off her perch on the milestone and trotted away toward the marsh in search of driftwood.

"If you remembered to put a knife in the toolbox," called her twin, "you can shave up some kindling yourself, and I won't have to stop."

"I most certainly did remember," Gilly called back. "Anyway, you know I can build a better fire than you, any time."

"She can, too," chuckled Pip when Gilly was out of hearing.

But Dan was thoughtful. In the space of seconds the twins had twice changed the subject. And he knew why. They had no intention of helping him in his revenge. They seemed to share, in fact, some powerful reason for keeping out of the feud between the Prides and the Bishops.

And the twins were afraid of the coming fog. If this were night, Dan was certain, neither one of them would be abroad in the marsh as they now were.

Gilly was soon back and had a fire blazing just beyond the skiff. Then she was off again for more driftwood. "Keep an eye on the fire," she called.

The boys finished painting the name and stood back to appraise their work. It looked good. The black letters stood out sharply against the white paint. Then, like the clanging of a gong, the meaning of the name came home to Dan. *Jinx.* The fire danced on the new paint, and the letters loomed large and hateful there in the clearing. He stood still a moment, remembering the Bishops with loathing. Then he grew aware of a quickening of the breeze, and with it something else. Something dreadful. The hair prickled on his scalp.

"Did you hear that?" he said sharply.

Pip looked up. "Hear what?"

But Gilly right then came clambering up onto the causeway, laden with driftwood. "Just look at all this!" she announced. "I couldn't see a smidgeon of wood anywhere. Then, bingo! I found a heap of it just below the mooring rock."

"Good," said Pip absently. He was still looking at Dan. "Is that what you mean?" The moaning of the foghorn came clearly in on the east wind.

Within hearing, Gilly piled driftwood beyond the reach of their fire. Dan nodded. There was no point in telling now what else he had heard—*the faraway music of a violin.* That must wait until he and Pip were alone again.

Gilly turned to Dan. "Remember that queer sign you found under the mooring rock? Like the one on the milestone?"

Dan looked at her. Gilly was on to something. "What about it?"

"That's where the driftwood was, all piled up at the tide line. When I pulled out some of the wood, I saw something."

"What was it?" Dan asked impatiently.

Gilly calmly fingered a straw-colored braid. "How much do you want to know?"

Dan glared at the girl and stifled the impulse to spank her.

"For gosh sake, Gil, tell us what you saw," said Pip calmly. "It won't be anything, Dan. It never is."

Gilly ignored her brother. "Give me first choice about where we go in the *Jinx,* and I'll tell you. I'm not telling Pip, though."

"Go chase yourself," laughed Pip. "We'll find out for ourselves. Come on, Dan!"

The boys started off at a good pace down the point road, but Gilly shot by like an arrow. Braids flying, she sprinted ahead of them down the causeway. Dan waited until they had nearly reached the bridge. Then he spurted past her and bounded like a deer down onto the mooring rock. Then he turned, quite simply, and helped her down.

Pip came up panting, the admiration in his blue eyes generous and warm. "Gosh, Dan, you never said you're a runner!"

Dan shook his head. "I'm not, really. I'm not the type." Somehow it no longer bothered him to admit this.

Gilly collapsed onto the rock beside them. "You're the type, all right, if you can beat me!"

"She's right, Dan. Nobody beats Gilly. I don't even try anymore. Wait till they see you next fall at track tryouts!"

Dan looked away. He might not be in York next fall. To his uncle he had become a burden, a troublemaker. But there was no need yet to tell the twins.

"Now for my discovery!" Gilly led the way from the mooring rock across the tumbled stones of the cave-in, and through a tangle of driftwood above the tide line.

"Now. Look right down in there."

The boys lay flat on the broken causeway beside Gilly, and gazed downward.

"Can't see a thing," stated Pip. "Just rocks."

But Dan made a shield of his hands and squinted into the moist darkness. Gradually the outlines of ancient stonework came clear. He seemed to be gazing upon the supporting wall of an arch within the causeway itself. "Yes, Gilly! I see." His voice, coming back to him from somewhere beneath, had an awed and hollow ring.

"I told you," said Gilly in triumph. "It's ruins, isn't it?"

"Ruins? What of?" Pip's voice, excited, was half lost in the echoes below.

They stared downward in silence. Then Gilly shrugged. "Since we can't move the causeway, we'll probably never find out. But except for me, nobody would have known it's there. That makes me feel spooky."

Pip said thoughtfully, "The colonists built defences against the Indians. Maybe this was something of that sort, and it fell into ruins. Then later on, they built the causeway right on top of it."

Reluctantly, Dan raised his face from the dim view of the past beneath him. He shook his head. "The colonial palisades were made of wood, I think. But these ruins—"

Suddenly Gilly scrambled to her feet. "Pip, it's gone," she said tersely.

"What's gone?" asked her brother, unconcerned.

"The jackknife. It's not in my pocket. I must have dropped it."

"Well, get humping and find it, then. I like that knife, Gil. I've had it for years."

Gilly kept her eyes on the water purling below them. "Pip, it wasn't your knife I put in the tool box. I couldn't find your knife."

Pip stared.

"I took Grandfather's."

"*Grandfather's!*" Her brother's calm face went red with anger. "My gosh, Gilly! You got rocks in your head?"

Gilly's eyes brimmed with tears. "You were in a hurry. You wouldn't wait."

Dan spoke up quickly. "Look here. I've got a knife in my room. It's rather a good one, and I shan't want it any more. If we can't find your grandfather's, you take mine."

"It isn't the *knife,*" said Gilly in a queer, strained voice. "It's just that it belonged to our grandfather."

Pip looked desperate. "It has his name on it." It was as if Pip had said, *It's the end of the world.*

"Let's get looking," he said heavily to Gilly. "We'll try the marsh first."

Dan rose to follow, but Pip glanced back. "Don't bother, Dan. Gilly and I'll find it."

"No trouble, really," said Dan, starting off the causeway.

Pip stopped at the edge of the marsh. "I said no, thanks," he said sharply.

For a moment the two friends stared at each other. The thing between them grew solid and cold, like a wall. Dan shrugged, as if it did not matter, and turned back to the ruin.

For some minutes he lay face-down, gazing blankly into the darkness. Below, the river purled and whispered, but the mystery of the hidden stonework had paled. What was this puzzle about a knife? Somehow it seemed to be tied up with the secret which the twins were keeping from him—some dark secret which would spoil things for the three of them.

A frightening half-thought took shape like a spectre below him, a thought that his mind balked at as a horse balks at a hurdle. He must follow the twins, must somehow put this black question into words, and learn the answer for himself!

Dan moved to rise from his hard perch. Then he froze, one arm still crooked beneath him. For the wind, gusting from the east, carried clearly the low sounds of a violin! Dan listened in horror. The music was wildly sweet, chilling. Strange cadences rose and fell in minor key, as if some unnatural violinist were playing a duet with the wind. Then the gust subsided. The sounds of the violin muted, and died away.

CHAPTER ELEVEN

Disaster

~~~~~~~~~~~~~~~~~~~~~~~~~~~~~~~~~~~~~~~

DAN went rigid with fear. Disaster was at hand! Where it would strike, and when, and whom, nobody knew. But he had heard the Fiddler, and trouble was coming! Unreasoning, Dan cowered against the causeway and terror took over.

Then the thought of Pip and Gilly drove him to his feet. He scanned the West Marsh—and breathed more easily. For the twins were safe, skirting a salt pond, searching heads down for the lost knife.

But the evil sound of the violin echoed through his head, and Dan moved to flee the causeway and its hidden ruin. Welcome or not, he would join the twins as soon as he could cover the distance that lay between them.

Later, Dan could not remember why he looked back. Perhaps it was the howl of the dog Caliban chained behind the cottage. Or perhaps it was the witch cackle of fire. But turning, he saw their little field ablaze and fire reaching greedily through the grass and into the brush!

Dan shouted to the twins, jabbing with a forefinger toward the clearing. Then he scrambled to the top of the causeway, seeing all too well the catastrophe to come. The grass fire licking the bushes would next sweep upward into the bone-dry pines around the chapel; then it would rage on into the wood lot, taking with it the hay barn and the outbuildings, and finally the house!

He called back to the twins, "Brooms inside the big barn!" Then he raced like the wind up the point road past the fire. He took the shortcut through the field and burst into the kitchen.

"Fire on the point!" he gasped.

Without wasting a word, Mrs. Corey headed straight for the telephone in the pantry.

Dan sped back to the barn. He attached Billy Ben's longest hose to the outlet nearest the chapel. Impatiently, he added all the extensions he could find. Once he caught a glimpse of Pip and Gilly, like twin furies, beating at the brush with their brooms. With sweat streaming into his eyes, Dan dragged the hose down the road. It reached, with only inches to spare, to the lower edge of the grove!

Desperate, he aimed the stream high into the brush. For long minutes there was no change. Flames crackled steadily into the bushes, reaching for the pines. The wind gusted from the east, swirling fog and smoke alike into his hot face. Flying embers scorched his clothing, and the hose became very heavy. Dan's arms were hot pipes thrusting out from his aching shoulders, and his eyes smarted with smoke and fatigue.

And then, little by little, the leading edge of the fire

began to fall back. The twins took heart, leaping to smother each new flame as it sprang up in the brush.

At one point, Mrs. Corey arrived with two large pails which she promptly filled with marsh water for the twins' brooms. She made a memorable figure as she bustled back and forth to the nearest ditch. Not for all the money in the world, Mrs. Corey had said, would she venture into the West Marsh during a fog. But for the love of Pride's Point there she went, not once but many times.

At last Dan laid down the hose and sat on a ledge by the road, his head sunk wearily between his aching shoulders. The water gushed at random onto the blackened land. Fire glowed still, but only in little islands of brush where it burned itself out. All the way from the marsh to the clean line of the pines, the ground lay black and ugly. But the pine grove and the chapel and all else were spared. And in a few weeks the point would be green again.

Mrs. Corey came puffing up, her dress wilted and sooty, her gray hair standing out like wires. She snorted with disgust, "*Now* the Department'll come poking along, now we got the fire out." She looked him over keenly. "You all right, Dan?"

He nodded.

"Well, I'm a worse sight than you, even—and the firemen coming!" She hurried toward the house. Dan looked after her with affection. Not a word had she said about their bonfire, still smouldering at the edge of the field. This duty then, would fall to his uncle, and it would be up to Dan to take the blame. For it was his boat, his responsibility. Besides, the twins were having trouble enough getting permission to come to Pride's. And they had worked like demons to control the fire.

Dan pulled himself to his feet and walked down the charred road to the field, looking for the twins. But they had gone back to their search for the knife. Just beyond the bridge Dan could make out the two fog-blurred figures in the West Marsh. Their burned brooms lay neatly beside the skiff.

He saw with relief that the little boat, being in the lee of the wind, remained untouched by the fire. He glanced toward the East Marsh to see if the Department was yet in sight. He saw instead the dim outline of his uncle's car!

Dan's heart fell. In the excitement he had forgotten that Uncle Julian planned to return early. But what a return. There would be no understanding talk between them today. Rather, his uncle would arrive to find that the boy he had taken into his home had now been criminally careless.

Dan waited where he was, disheveled and shivering and soaked to the skin. It seemed forever before his uncle came down the hill toward him. His glance took in the long hose line, the blackened field, the skeletal brush still smoking; and his gaunt face grew sterner than usual. His eyes passed over the skiff, came to rest on the newly-painted name.

He turned then to face the boy. The deep eyes looked hopeless, and Dan's heart was heavy. How could he explain the fire? Even more important, how could he now make his uncle understand that he wanted his friendship more than anything else in the world?

Haltingly, Dan said, "My friends and I—" He swallowed and started again. "The fire was a mistake. We were working on the skiff and made a bonfire to get warm. The wind came up, and the grass caught fire and the fire spread into the brush."

"Anyone can make a mistake," said Uncle Julian after a moment. Then he asked, "Where are these 'friends' of yours now?" His voice was as bitter as medicine.

Dan looked helplessly toward the West Marsh. Pip and Gilly were nowhere to be seen. "I don't know, sir. But the fire wasn't their fault. They worked terribly hard to help put it out."

His uncle grunted. "And then left you to face the music."

"No. They just—had to leave," said Dan loyally, wishing he knew the reason why.

"But they are not guilty of anything except a careless mistake. Is that it?"

Dan nodded.

Something—was it approval?—flickered in the shadowed eyes. "What about yourself, Dan? Not guilty either?"

Dan smiled tentatively, and understanding began to glow like a spark in the wind.

There was the roar of heavy wheels on the driveway above. Then loud voices shattered the silence between them. Down the drive between the willows came several men, helmeted and booted. Dan glanced at his uncle. The curtain had come down over the troubled face. They waited together.

The men stopped before them. They looked at Julian Pride and his nephew with watchful eyes.

Dan cried out silently to his uncle: *Be friendly, like Billy Ben. Show them you don't despise them!*

But Julian Pride remained behind his curtain, aloof and proud. "Thank you for coming, gentlemen. But as you can see, the fire is already out."

The man wearing the Chief's hat scratched his head defensively. "We came just as soon's Amy Corey called us."

"Thank you very much." Uncle Julian's tone was final.

"If it's okay with you, we'll look around just the same. Make sure everything's all right," said the Chief evenly. He gave directions to the men, then he turned to Dan. The boy was suddenly aware of his sooty face and hands, the scorched places on his clothes. "Just what happened out here, Boy?"

Dan hesitated, coloring. He began to feel guilty of some crime.

Uncle Julian said coldly, "My nephew made a bonfire and it got into the brush by accident. He helped extinguish it himself. No damage was done at all."

The Chief took a small notebook from his pocket. "Just for the record. Your nephew, Daniel Pride," he said slowly as he wrote. "An accident, you say."

Uncle Julian snapped, "I not only *say* it. It was exactly that. An accident."

The Chief looked up in surprise. He had the look of a man determined not to be pushed beyond his patience. "Nobody claimed it wasn't, did they?" He even made an attempt at humor. "No one else involved? Like, for instance, the Fiddler?"

The men laughed uneasily. Dan closed his mind to the

unearthly music he had heard down at the causeway. Uncle Julian looked at the Chief as if he had not spoken at all.

Embarrassed, the Chief snapped his notebook shut. His voice was taut. "I hope young Dan here has learned a good lesson. Anyone gets careless with fires, takes a big chance in a drought like this." He turned abruptly. "All okay, boys?"

"All okay." The men were clomping back up the road.

Dan drew a deep breath. Now they would go away. But the wall between the Prides and the townspeople had grown higher than ever. If only he were clever, could find the words to break down the wall!

A flash of green among the trees, and Billy Ben burst into the group like sun on the clouds. "Howdy, Chief," he shouted. "Hi, Ed. What's the matter, late again? Afternoon, sir," he added to Julian Pride.

The Chief snorted good-naturedly. "What do you mean, 'late again'?"

The man named Ed added, "They just wasn't any fire worth coming way out here for, Billy."

Julian Pride stiffened. "I'm sure Mrs. Corey would not have called you if she hadn't thought it necessary."

Ed shrugged in apology. "*Could* of been a bad fire, sir. Fact is, we sort of expected a bad one, what with this fog." The men glanced significantly at Billy Ben.

Then Dan saw something else: the sudden narrowing of Billy Ben's eyes as he read the name freshly painted on the skiff. *Jinx.* Ed followed his look, nudged the man beside him, and they both stared. *Jinx.* Dan would have given anything to blot out the name; but the damage was done. Now there would be more gossip in York, not only about Pride's Point and the fog, and the fire that could have been a bad one, but also about himself. It would be pointed out that in the fog disaster had come close. And it had come through young Dan Pride.

Uncle Julian said crisply, "My nephew and I are sorry you came out here for nothing. Thank you again for coming." It was dismissal. But Dan was thinking jubilantly: "*My nephew and I.*" Suddenly he was no longer afraid of these men.

Then Billy Ben's great voice filled the air, genial and hearty. "How about something special from the wine cellar, sir, for the boys to take back?"

Uncle Julian stared in surprise at his yard man. Dan wondered, was Billy Ben being officious, or merely bumbling? Even a generous person does not offer another man's property.

Billy Ben shrugged. "I mean, sir, it's a Fiddler's fog, and something *could* have happened. For all they knew, it could have happened right here at Pride's Point."

Dan held his breath. Now his uncle would put in its place this whole nonsense about a Fiddler's fog and the trouble it brought, just as he would put Billy Ben in his place.

But Uncle Julian did neither. After a moment he nodded, wearily.

"Thanks, sir!" In a pleasant mockery, Billy Ben ducked his head toward his employer.

The men followed him up the driveway in a burst of good spirits. It would be Billy Ben whom they would thank for their gifts. And the yard man, as if he himself were master of Pride's, would accept their thanks.

"Dan," said his uncle. "How about a cup of tea?" There
was a wry note of kinship in his voice. He and Dan had
somehow lost a match, but at least they had stood together.

Dan smiled. "I'd like that very much, sir. First, though,
I'd better clean up the hose and things."

"That," said Uncle Julian flatly, "is still Billy Ben's
job."

They walked together up the road past the skiff. Behind
them the Witches' Bridge slept shrouded in the thick mist.
A Fiddler's fog, and there really had been no disaster at
all, Dan thought triumphantly. Only a grass fire that
could have happened to anyone.

"Thank you for keeping my friends' names out of this,"
he said.

His uncle gave him a quizzical look. "Since you had not
mentioned their names, I could hardly report them, could
I?" There was a touch of conspiracy in the remark, and
Dan's heart sang. It began to look as though he might
have a family after all.

Now it would be easy to talk with Uncle Julian. "I mean
to find my grandfather's briefcase," he would say, "if it's
the last thing I do." And Uncle Julian would not scorn to
help him. Together they would discuss possibilities, explore the old house and the marsh, find the case, and
prove the Bishops false. Then the foolish stories about the
Prides would end for all time!

"Uncle Julian," Dan began, "there are some things I've
been wanting to talk to you about."

"Good. Save them for tea." His uncle sounded pleased.
He stooped to pick up something from the charred grass
beside the road. "Someone's jackknife. A very nice one."

Carefully, he wiped away the soot with his handkerchief.

"It belongs to Pip's grandfather," said Dan eagerly. "Gilly was awfully uspet when she lost it."

Uncle Julian was staring oddly at the knife, and his face had gone gray. He spoke very quietly. "So you broke faith with me, Dan. You—and the Bishops." He handed Dan the knife.

Dan, suddenly fearful, took it. Pip's and Gilly's knife, with their grandfather's name branded into the handle.

Philip Bishop, Dan read. *Philip Bishop.* For one sick moment Dan's mind stuck with astonishment. Then it began to run forward and back again, like a frenzied dog. *Pip and Gilly were Bishops.* That was their secret. They had lied to him. They had listened to his talk about the Fiddler, and they had spread rumors, and they had laughed at his uncle and at him behind his back. They had run away and let him take the blame for the fire.

His face darkened. Dan looked up from the knife to match his hatred with his uncle's. But Uncle Julian was no longer beside him. He was just entering the house, his thin figure stooped now, no longer upright. He looked like a man who was very tired.

The thought came slowly, with a crushing force: *his uncle believed that Dan had knowingly made friends with the Bishops!* For a Pride, this was the crime of crimes. Unless Dan could explain the chain of events, this was the end of friendship between him and his uncle.

He started to run toward the house. But when he reached the beeches, he stopped. Explain? he thought bitterly. How could he ask Uncle Julian to believe that Dan never knew his best friends were Bishops? How could he prove that he himself had been tricked?

In a black rage, Dan drew back his arm and flung the hateful knife with all his strength toward the West Marsh. It disappeared without a sound into the mist.

Slowly, he crossed the lawn under the dripping beeches. He headed for his room because there was no other place to go. The smell of burned grass was acrid in his nostrils. The east wind blew strong and chill now, and the foghorn sounded very near. Steadily, the fog had closed in, blotting out everything except the crest of Pride's Island.

It was a Fiddler's fog, all right. And it had brought, after all, disaster.

CHAPTER TWELVE

Billy Ben

～～～～～～～～～～～～～～～～～

DAN sat at his window and stared out at the empty bridge. One corner of the sky still glowed with the sunset. Against it the bridge arched black and bare.

It had been a long week. Since the fire, Uncle Julian had taken himself back into his other world of dark thought and silence. Dinners they shared under the fierce eye of the old Puritan. But they rarely spoke. Pain twisted inside Dan at the thought of their growing friendship, and how suddenly it died as they read the name on the twins' lost jackknife. As for Pip and Gilly, Dan slammed his mind shut on them. But his hatred of the Bishops had grown furiously like the fire on the point, consuming everything before it.

"For goodness' sake, Dan. What you sitting here in the dark for? Trying to ruin your eyes?" Mrs. Corey bustled in and turned on Dan's lights, bringing cheerfulness into the room. "Here's some clothes of yours, mended all nice."

Dan thanked her and pretended to read as she put

things away. But she did not leave when the chore was done. Instead she plumped herself down on the window seat. She has something on her mind, thought Dan, and she's come to get it off.

"There he is now," she said suddenly.

His uncle was walking slowly toward the house along the twilit road. It seemed to Dan that he looked thinner, and somehow uncertain.

"He's low again, for some reason," said the housekeeper.

Dan said nothing.

"Seems funny not to see that poor dog with him," she went on.

Dan looked away. "Billy Ben thought the dog should be tied up. He tried to attack us one day last week."

"Well, Billy Ben better mind his own business. He's been getting pretty important lately, seems to me." Mrs. Corey looked sharply at Dan. "But 'tisn't the dog that's eating your uncle. It's you." She waited, her back grimly straight, her face kindly. "What's the trouble, Dan?"

Dan hesitated. Then the need to talk welled up inside him. "My uncle thinks I've lied to him. I made friends with a couple of children from one of the shacks on the mainland, I thought. We worked on the skiff together. They—seemed to be the best friends I ever had." Dan's voice was heavy with bitterness. It sounded like his uncle's.

"Well, who were they?" But Dan could tell from her face that she had already guessed.

"Pip and Gilly Cole."

"Ann Bishop's young ones!" Then Mrs. Corey lashed out

with fury. "That's just like those Bishops, not to let on who they were! The pups are as bad as the dogs! You just keep clear of 'em, Dan!"

He said dully, "Every day since the fire they come back to the bridge. They came again today. But I never go down, and they never come up here. After a while, they always go away."

" 'Course they won't come here!" cried Mrs. Corey with lively horror. "If they ever dared, I'd give 'em a good piece of my mind!"

Dan stared toward the bridge. It was a stone arm separating the two families.

"Didn't you tell your Uncle Julian?"

Dan shook his head. "He wouldn't have believed me. He hates me, you know."

The silence grew long. Then her voice softened. "Maybe it just looks that way, Dan."

"And now it's too late," said Dan, hardly hearing her.

The housekeeper shook her head as if Prides were beyond her.

She changed the subject briskly. "You put the skiff in the water yet?"

Dan cheered somewhat. "Two days ago. And yesterday I rowed down the river a short way. I saw a bittern."

"I've heard 'em around. Billy Ben'll get 'em with his bird gun, come fall." She chatted on about the youth's prowess as a hunter.

Dan was not listening. The bittern had reminded him hatefully of Pip and Gilly. Yet he would not soon forget it. He had come upon it in the black-grass fringe of a little island. The bird was standing motionless in a curious, leaning posture, her bill pointing upward, her streaked buffs and browns blending with the dead grass. As Dan moved eagerly, she left this deception and spread her feeble wings and hissed. Before he rowed away, Dan caught a glimpse of the nest, a thin flat platter of dry grasses. And he had felt a stirring of brotherhood toward the bird, and a wonder that Billy Ben would take pride in killing her.

"Does the skiff leak?" Mrs. Corey was asking.

"Like a sieve," Dan admitted, smiling a little. "But she's beginning to tighten up."

Mrs. Corey nodded approvingly. "She, for a boat. Pretty soon you'll be talking normal, like the rest of us. But you be turrible careful, now, fooling around in that marsh." And the housekeeper, shaking her head, said goodnight and took herself away.

Dan stared out at the darkness. Perhaps she would convince Uncle Julian that it was the twins, not Dan, who had been guilty of deception. Then his uncle would send them away, and Dan would not need to watch them come again to the bridge, with the hatred sick inside him.

But it turned out to be Billy Ben who got rid of the twins.

The days inched by hot and cloudless, and haymaking time was upon them. One morning, stripped to the waist under the broiling sun, Dan helped Billy Ben with the summer's first haying. With a feeling of relief, he told the whole story about the fire, and Philip Bishop's lost knife.

"Bishops!" Billy Ben spat out the word as if he had said, "Poison!" "They could have set the whole island on fire. I'm surprised they haven't tried it before."

"The fire was no more their fault than mine. But they

never once told me that they're Bishops," Dan added bitterly.

"That's the Bishops for you!" nodded Billy Ben. "And don't be too sure that fire wasn't their fault. They didn't stick around, did they?"

Dan said nothing.

"Don't worry, Danny Boy, they won't bother us after today." Billy Ben winked, and Dan had the feeling that he would somehow take care of everything. The sun-filled hours sped by, and the comradeship between them grew strong.

Dan watched closely as Billy Ben guided the tractor alongside the main ditches which, if cut too closely, could snap a tractor over onto its side. Before the morning was over, he had learned to operate the tractor himself. Soon an ever-growing part of the great East Marsh lay in golden rows behind them. They took only minutes for lunch, then Billy Ben hurried him back to the marsh.

"If we work hard," said Billy Ben, "we can finish this part by four. Then I aim to get at that foundation."

Dan was growing tired and his skin felt strange and tight, but he did not complain. Instead he said loyally, "Mrs. Corey says you're always working."

Billy Ben threw back his head and laughed. "She'd be surprised how hard I work!" And he swept Dan into a friendly tussle that ended with the two of them deep in the mown hay, and Dan helpless with laughter.

It was a wonderful, hard-working, blistering, boisterous day. At last, Dan felt, the hired man had accepted him as an equal. Late in the afternoon, Billy Ben even shared his dreams for Pride's Point.

"One way or another, Danny Boy, I'm going to get me a

fistful of money. Then I'm off to see the world, blessed if I'm not. And when I get back I'll be in charge of Pride's, you see if I'm not. By then your uncle'll need a full-time manager, just like my daddy used to be." He broke off, his round face shining. "Then what I won't do with this place— You see all that marshland over past the new road?"

Dan looked. The great East Marsh reached shimmering out of sight into the distance. Pride land. Dan felt a stirring of loyalty.

"I'll sell out—get your uncle to sell out."

"Sell out!" Dan stared in surprise.

"Make the marsh really pay. Land's money, these days. The bird hunters'll gobble it up for cottage lots. And up near the highway, that's good industrial land. A few tons of fill here and there, and we got ourself a pot of money!"

Dan did not follow all of Billy Ben's high plans. He only knew that he was happier than he had been since the disaster on the point a fortnight ago. He thought of the twins scarcely at all that day.

When, late in the afternoon, he saw the slight figure of a boy slowly crossing the old causeway from the mainland, anger beat hot and proud in his head. So Gilly had finally given up! And why didn't Pip, too, leave him alone?

Billy Ben followed his look. "Time to call it a day, Danny Boy. Let's go get us a Bishop!"

They left the East Marsh then, and Billy Ben parked the tractor in the barnyard. "You stay out of this," he told Dan genially.

From the cool darkness of the barn, Dan watched him

go, down between the willows to the point road. In a few minutes Billy Ben would send Pip away for good. As he waited, Dan heard the baying of the great dog chained behind the cottage. He shuddered, thankful again for Billy Ben. He tried to forget that Uncle Julian had never troubled himself to restrain a killer.

The minutes dragged past, and Dan's back began to burn. He noticed nearby a sack of ready-mix cement not yet opened. Billy Ben must still have some digging left to do at the chapel. Then Dan had an idea. Billy Ben was trying to help him. While Dan waited, he could do some of Billy Ben's unfinished work on the foundation! Pleased with the thought, he found a spade and hurried down the path to the chapel.

The low sun cast spidery shapes of evergreens across the chapel door. The windows stared blindly out of the shadows. Dan shook off his apprehension and studied the work before him. Parts of the old foundation were in need of cement, and Billy Ben was digging a ditch around the entire base before making the necessary repairs.

Dan stepped into the trench and began to dig. He noticed something that interested him: the ancient masonry supporting the chapel looked much like the stonework under the causeway. It was masterly work in both places, built to endure.

Dan dug quietly and as rapidly as he could, intending to surprise Billy Ben. But soon his sunburn became unbearable. He was taking off his shirt when he heard swift steps on the path above him. Billy Ben stared down. He looked enormous, crouched as he was against the sky, and his voice was loud with anger.

"Give me that spade!"

Dan stared up in amazement.

"I said give me that spade!" Billy Ben shouted.

Bewildered, Dan handed up the spade.

"Now get out of there, you little runt!"

Dan scrambled up from the trench, unable to look away from the flushed face, the hard eyes. There was no friendship now, not even the pretense of it. Billy Ben had a strange, violent look, like the look of the dog Caliban. Why, thought Dan with vast surprise, *Billy Ben hates me.*

"When I need your help, I'll ask for it. And when I don't ask for it, you stay out of my hair. You got that?" Billy Ben half raised one arm, the back of his great fist toward Dan's face.

The boy's mouth closed tightly. He stood woodenly beside the trench.

Billy Ben's large round eyes explored the stonework which Dan had just exposed. Then he seemed to relax. "I'm sorry, Danny Boy. But there's a right way to do these things, you know. Besides—" he made a helpless gesture, "that uncle of yours will have my head if you get blisters again. It's bad enough you got that sunburn." He grinned companionably, and waited.

Dan did not believe Billy Ben. He could feel the angry blood pounding in his head, and his jaws ached from holding back dangerous words. His one wish was to get away. But he must not go, not yet. First he would have to reassure Billy Ben. He forced a smile. "That's all right, really."

"You sure?"

"Really. I should have asked you first."

Billy Ben's smile was indulgent. "Well, you run along and get something on that sunburn. —And how about keeping your aches and pains to yourself for a change, Danny Boy? Keep me out of hot water, okay?"

Dan nodded.

"Good enough!" said Billy Ben heartily. "And you can forget about your fine friend. He's not your friend anymore," he laughed.

"Thanks very much," Dan said clearly. It was safe to go now. He walked slowly away. He could feel Billy Ben's eyes probing into his back. He was relieved when the path turned among the pines and hid him from view.

Then his legs went liquid. He seemed to be afire from the waist up, a bonfire walking unevenly on liquid legs. Dan leaned against a rock, his head pounding. *Billy Ben is my enemy, not my friend,* he thought. Then the boy's eyes opened wide with astonishment. He's hated me ever since I came. He hates me, and he means to do me harm. But as long as he still thinks he's fooling me, I'll be safe enough from him . . .

Dan's thoughts ran feverishly on. Why was Billy Ben so angry when Dan helped dig at the foundation? Could it be that he was, in fact, searching for something—that all his "projects" had been merely a cover-up for some great search?

Then Dan knew: *Billy Ben, too, was seeking the briefcase!* He had not, that first year, given up at all. Now he was searching the entire island, bit by bit.

But why? Did he hope to win Julian Pride's favor by finding the lost papers? No, because Billy Ben had shown little love for his employer. Dan struggled to understand.

Could a hatred of the Bishops have led him into the search? The boy shook his head hopelessly. Billy Ben's warnings to keep away from the Bishops did not show any strong dislike for them. Also, why should he act so secretive, if exposing the Bishops were the only reason for his search?

Out of the welter of new thoughts, one fact stood out boldly. *Billy Ben, too, was searching for the briefcase.* But why? His reason must be a terribly important one. Dan remembered the blotched fury in Billy Ben's face, the brutal knotting of his fist.

At that moment the sounds of the spade stopped. Silence filled and threatened the woods.

Heedless of the noise he made, Dan fled through the woods and across the lawn and into the house.

CHAPTER THIRTEEN

Down the River

~~~~~~

DAN took the back stairs two at a time and sought refuge in his room. He flung himself on the window seat and stared out toward the hidden chapel, his heart pounding and his thoughts racing.

For whatever reason, Billy Ben was searching for the lost papers—Pride papers. And somehow Dan knew that if Billy Ben found them he would keep his find secret from Julian Pride, even as he was keeping his long search secret.

Dan made a decision. He would keep away from Billy Ben in order to hide his own quest. But he, not the hired man, would be the first to find his grandfather's papers! And he could not wait any longer for a talk with Uncle Julian. He must start without his help.

His purpose clear, Dan sought out Mrs. Corey. She looked up scowling from her magazine.

"I've been thinking about my grandfather's briefcase—" Dan began.

"Don't," she said curtly. "There's things we're not meant to know on this earth, Dan. Bad things. You leave 'em alone."

"But did my grandfather have time to bury the case, do you think?" Dan persisted. "What about walls or foundations around Pride's? Did Billy Ben ever—?"

"Now you just let sleepy dogs lie," she snapped, "or heads'll shake and tongues'll wag, and worse'n that will happen!" Then she eyed Dan suspiciously. "You sure you don't have a good sunburn under that shirt?"

Dan moved his shoulders painfully, and his head throbbed with the motion. Tomorrow. Tomorrow he would start his search in earnest.

"Billy Ben's got some sunburn cream down at the cottage. You go get some, if your back's anything like your nose." And Mrs. Corey marched off to the kitchen.

At that point, Billy Ben's cottage was the last place in the world that Dan would choose to visit. But hours later he wished mightily that he had taken her advice. Sleepless, he turned onto his stomach, unable to bear even a sheet across his blistering back. He felt ill and feverish, and never more alone in his life. His uncle had lost faith in him. The twins had betrayed him. Even Billy Ben had turned into an enemy—an enemy searching ruthlessly for Pride papers. And why? *Why?*

He left his bed and pulled on his pants. Heavy-eyed, he opened the window wide. He stared out with awe and delight. It was the time when full moon and flood tide combine to give back the marshland to the sea. All the way to the opposite shore the West Marsh was a broad, bright gulf. Somewhere in the east the moon was rising, and long fingers of mist reached over the high water. A million stars glimmered in the sky and shone back from the brimming marsh. Above and below, the night was filled with unearthly beauty.

The cool air streamed like a river over Dan's hot face, bringing in the scent of new hay and salt marsh and Billy Ben's roses below. Peace began to flow through him like a deep tide. And with the peace came remembrance. The portrait eyes of Samuel the witch, black and blazing, reminding him of his promise. The briefcase.

The boy stirred restlessly. Over that same bridge one night long ago another Dan Pride had come. And somewhere was hidden the proof that he *had* completed his business with the Bishops. Somewhere. But where?

Dan could rule out the house and the outbuildings. They had long since been combed by the family, and later by Billy Ben. The marsh itself he could cross off. For anything hidden there would now be buried in mud, or long ago lost in the tide. He could forget the gardens and orchard. Billy Ben's projects had taken care of these. Now the hired man was clearly placing his hopes in the old chapel. But why the foundation?

Dan rose from the window. He must find out for himself. Now, while Billy Ben slept, he must go to the chapel.

He moved quietly on bare feet down the steep back stairs, and out into the starry night. He kept to the shadows of the beeches until he reached the road, then he ran swiftly down to the point.

In the full moonlight the chapel was guarded by a spectral army of shadows.

Grimly, Dan followed the path to the front wall and stepped down into the trench. He examined the entire ditch, but nowhere, either here or in the ancient wall, was there any hint of a hiding place. Billy Ben had found nothing up to this point, Dan was sure of it. The chapel rose silently above him. If it hid a secret, he would not learn it tonight. He was free to go back to the house now.

Then reluctantly, Dan knew there was one thing more to be done. The foundation wall interested Billy Ben. If he went inside the chapel perhaps he could discover the reason why. Dan forced himself to enter. The door opened unwillingly, as before. He held panic at bay, refusing to think or to feel.

The moonlight shone through the trees outside and barred the room like a prison. The chapel was silent, and empty. No door leading down to a cellar. No stairs leading to a loft. Nothing. There was nothing here. A flood of relief brought his breath hoarsely into his throat, and Dan turned and fled down the path, leaving behind him the black pines and the empty chapel, its great door yawning wide.

At the point road he hesitated. If he went back to the house it would be as before: a paining back and a lonely, wakeful night. Dan turned the other way to the causeway. He had a strange idea that here near the bridge, in the deep of the night, he might learn what had happened to his grandfather. And he might learn why Billy Ben sought Pride papers so feverishly.

The *Jinx* rested on the mooring rock, inches above the flood tide. Her sides glistened in the moonlight, and Dan remembered Pip's placid face as he bent over his work. He remembered, too, with a surge of pain, the quick secret looks between the twins.

On a whim, Dan eased the skiff into the high water, leaving the painter tied to the stake in the rock. Then he climbed aboard and sat down, and the mist rose from the river and lay cool upon his back. He wished he had brought the oars from the barn. Then he would leave Pride's Point and go—somewhere down the river. Where, no one would know. No one would care.

Dan felt wholly alone. The strange high tide and the late hour made the place seem alien and unfamiliar. No one knew he was here. If he were to call out, no one would hear him.

In that instant, Dan was aware of something waiting nearby. There was the sense of eyes watching him, a whisper of motion on the causeway above. Then, against the moon, he made out the black shape of the dog! The great head was lowered and baleful. Dan could not see the yellow eyes, but he sensed that Caliban was waiting for a sudden motion on his part—waiting to attack.

Dan looked frantically about him. Clearly he could not escape the animal over the mooring rock. There was only one other way to go. With trembling fingers he reached out and untied the painter. The *Jinx* drifted outward toward the current, gathering speed.

A sudden motion above him, and Caliban leaped awkwardly down onto the rock. Then he hurled his crippled body into the backwater. Dan watched in horror. The dog was swimming powerfully beside him! Together they moved into the current and on under the bridge, the skiff and the boy, with the dog close by.

In spite of his fear Dan saw something strange about the beast. Deformed and ugly on land, here in the water Caliban was in his element. Here he became a thing of beauty, his great body relaxed, his motions strong and sure.

Now they were approaching the landing rock. Dan knew that somehow he must steer the skiff onto the ledge. Then, with a groan, he saw that the landing was covered by the tide. If the flat-bottomed skiff passed over the ledge, it would next move out into midstream where the current raced through the Gut. How he could then manage the boat, or what the dog might do, Dan dared not guess.

With nightmare speed the bridge fell behind. Now the landing was seconds away. Now it was below them, with a hushing sound of drowned thatch. Instinctively, Dan plunged his arms deep into the water, grasped the thatch swirling beneath. He held tight with both hands, praying the grass would hold. The stern swung around and the dog came sharply against it. He was panting heavily now, his great paws flailing at the skiff.

Then, with a wrench, the thatch pulled free and the skiff sprang back into the tide. Now Dan knew he must stay with the boat for there could be no escape on foot. The marshland was flooded from shore to shore, and the salt ponds lay hidden by the tide.

The dog still followed. Now they were in mid-river moving swiftly together, and Dan saw what effort it cost him to keep on.

In all that vast wetland, there was no sound except the ripple of water against the boat, and an occasional splash of the tiring paws. Dan stared numbly at the animal. Uncle Julian loved Caliban, and the dog was going to drown. Here again would be another tragedy, and on Dan's account!

These thoughts struggled against the boy's deep fear of the dog. Suddenly, without conscious thought, he was at the stern. He hooked his leg over the thwart and reached far forward. Then his hands were in the rough fur. He could feel the great muscles tense as the dog gathered his strength for the final effort. For a few seconds the fate of the skiff hung in the balance. Then Caliban was in the boat, his feet braced on the bottom. He shook his coat in an explosion of moon-bright spray and sank down, panting heavily. The skiff leveled itself and moved on down river. Then Caliban placed his great head on Dan's knee and wearily closed his eyes.

Something stung behind the boy's eyelids, and he began to understand. When Caliban came to him in the barn he had brought a cautious offer of friendship. And the day Billy Ben hurled the brick, the dog's hatred had been directed at the hired man, not at Dan. Then in the long days since, when Caliban had been tied, even Uncle Julian had abandoned him. No wonder he had howled in his loneliness. And the dog's ribs were too prominent. Dan suspected that Billy Ben had not troubled to feed him properly. He ran a light hand over the animal's side, and Caliban gazed back with devotion.

The moon followed them into the swift waters of the Gut and beyond, where the river broadened and curved through the marshland. They passed silently under the east causeway bridge. Now and then a night bird cried. Once a fox barked from an inland hill. And one by one, the little sleeping islands slipped by. Sooner or later they would reach the harbor. From there he and the dog could make their way back to Pride's over the east causeway.

The *Jinx* swept around a broad bend. Here the river was divided by a high wooded island. Dan gazed in wonder at the steep bank above him. He could see in the moonlight the tough little junipers, the bayberry that crowded down to the water.

Then without warning, the skiff struck on a ledge and sent Dan sprawling off the thwart against Caliban. The dog sprang ashore, and instinctively the boy scrambled after him. Just as the skiff swung back into the current, he grasped it by the bow and dragged it beyond the reach of the river.

They had hit an outthrusting arm of granite not unlike the ledge at Pride's. The tide moved with force against this barrier, swirling around it and thence on to the sea.

Here Dan stood, unsure of what to do. He rubbed the dog's ugly head, and Caliban pushed against him with the force of a small horse. Then the dog went rigid. Dan heard it, too: slow footsteps coming toward them through the thicket. The dog's head lowered. He growled deep in his throat and the coarse hair rose stiffly along his spine.

Dan clutched the fur on Caliban's shoulders. For now he remembered what island this must be. It was the one inhabited island in the vast East Marsh, the one which Pip had said they might "run into" if they rode the tide down to the sea.

The skiff had carried him and the dog to Lamie's Island!

CHAPTER FOURTEEN

Lamie

~~~~~~

THEY waited, the dog bristling and defensive, the boy stiff with apprehension. Here was the madman coming, and no escape from him. Perhaps, thought Dan wildly, this was to be his doom for venturing so boldly into the marsh by night!

Then out of the bayberry thicket stepped Lamie. He was a little, stooped old man, with a body so spare that he seemed no bigger than Gilly. He had a shock of fine white hair that shone like beach grass in the moonlight, and beneath it a face so serene and kind that it seemed to Dan like the face of a good child.

When he saw the boy and the dog he bowed with great dignity and broke into a smile that set the wrinkles dancing in his face. "Welcome! Welcome!" he said in a voice too deep for the size of him. "Welcome to the loveliest island in the East Marsh. Beloved of the Indians, it was, and cleared and cultivated by good people who all have left, long since. And now, as you see," the old man made a

138

sweeping gesture that was both proud and apologetic, "inhabited by only me, Lamie."

Dan stared, speechless. But Caliban's tail began to stir.

"Please come," said Lamie. He turned, and in the next instant was out of sight in the thicket.

Dan seemed to have no will of his own. Numbly, with legs like rubber, he followed the old man, and the dog padded behind.

The path wound upward past cellar walls and old lilac trees. It mounted a moonlit slope dark with unripe blueberries and led at last to a shack made, it seemed, entirely of driftwood and perched at the top of the island under a great thorn tree. Beyond, Dan caught a glimpse of the vast East Marsh, drowned in a silver sea. In a little cove below, a lobster boat lay tied alongside a rickety wharf. Over boat and cove and marsh beyond, streamed the moonlight.

"I see you love the marsh, and that is good."

Dan started. He had not seen the old man, seated as he was in the shade of the thorn tree.

Lamie chuckled. "Sit down, my boy. There is nothing to be afraid of. The earth and the night are kind." The hermit spoke very deliberately, as if he were out of the habit of speaking. His talk had the ring of ancient books read and reread, rather than of words spoken in the busy world of men.

Dan took the chair opposite Lamie's, a high-backed throne of wood with the bark left on. It was surprisingly comfortable and Dan leaned his burned back carefully against it. With a deep sigh, Caliban stretched out beside him and closed his eyes.

Lamie excused himself and returned with a small canister in one hand. In the other he held a bottle by its neck and two curious glass mugs, their handles ringing his fingers. With simply ceremony, he placed these things on the rough table between them.

"If you will permit me, this salve will be a comfort." So saying, the old man gently soothed onto Dan's fiery back and shoulders a cream both cool and fragrant, smelling of bayberries. "My mother made such ointment as this, and her mother before her."

Dan nodded. Already the fire seemed to be seeping out of his back.

"They have not gone, you know, those good people. You see them in the ditches dug in the marsh, and in the cellar holes below. Aye," nodded Lamie, pronouncing the word in the ancient, two-syllable fashion, "and you see them in the white roses that grow wild, now, on all our islands. They brought the roses with them when they came, three hundred years ago and half a world away."

The old hands were gentle and healing, and the deep, musing voice went on. "They are still here, our first people. All still here, with Lamie." With grave courtesy, the ancient man poured a dark red liquid into the mugs and handed one to Dan. "This is elderberry shrub, made from my finest berries. I fetched it out of the cellar when I saw you coming."

"Weren't you asleep?" Dan asked in wonder. "It must be past midnight."

"No, my son. To sleep on such a night would be a crime."

Dan nodded politely, as if the thought were a common one. He sipped his drink. It glowed as red as fire, and it was cold, delicious.

"Do you live here alone?" he asked.

His host nodded. "Alone, aye. But not lonely. There is a difference. A man at peace with his thoughts is not lonely anywhere."

Dan understood. Uncle Julian was the loneliest man Dan had ever known. He must be as lonely in Boston as at Pride's Point.

"How do you live?" he asked curiously.

"Off the land and the sea, my son," said Lamie. "I fish and lobster and clam, all year 'round. What I can't use I sell in York, and what I can't raise, I buy. Down there, you see my garden."

In the moonlight Dan saw the corn and peas and beans standing already higher than Billy Ben's. And beyond, a tiny orchard sloped to the marsh's edge.

"I use our modern methods, my son," said Lamie, "for it is a foolish man who lives in the past. But I never forget the secrets of the Indians, too." He winked as if they both knew that the time between the little island's past and its present amounted to nothing at all. Lamie seemed ageless. He could as well have lived three hundred years ago, or a hundred years hence.

But he was surely not crazy. If Lamie is different from others, Dan told himself, it is in his strange way of living and, yes, in his love of the world.

Dan hesitated. Then he asked, "You must have heard

the old stories of the Fiddler and his curse. Do you believe them?"

"No, not I," said Lamie thoughtfully. "Sometimes,
though, when the wind is east, I, too, have heard the
sound of music. But I have heard this only near the old
bridge which they say is haunted."

"Do you think the bridge is haunted?" urged Dan.

The old man nodded sadly. "Haunted it is, in many
ways. But a body would do well to look for some natural
cause, not for the spirit of a good man who left his marsh
long before you came here, Dan Pride."

"You know my name?" said Dan, surprised.

There was a world of kindness in Lamie's faded eyes. "I
knew you the instant I saw you by the skiff. You had the
look of your grandfather, who was a gentleman. You were
afraid, but you did not run. Instead you looked very
fierce, you and that beast of yours," smiled Lamie.

"Caliban belongs to my uncle," said Dan. The dog
moved his tail sleepily, and Lamie shook his head in pity.
But whether for Julian Pride or for Caliban, Dan did not
know.

"Did you know my grandfather?" he asked.

"I knew him well," said Lamie softly. "Daniel Pride was
a hero and a martyr like his ancestor, Samuel, and I admired him for that. And he loved his fellowmen. For that
I loved him."

Dan waited to hear more, his back nearly free of pain,
his body warmed as much by the beauty of the moon's
glow as by Lamie's elderberry shrub.

"I did many a journeyman's job for Dan Pride, working
on his marshlands and in his gardens. He was a great man,

without pretense and without pretention. His foreman,
Elder Corey, was not such a man, but I think your grandfather did not know this. He saw only loyalty in Elder
Corey, as all good men see only good in others." Lamie
leaned his silvery head back against the chair and closed
his eyes. His voice went musically on and Dan, his eyelids
heavy, seemed to hear each word as one would hear a
bell, every deep, slow note crystal-clear.

"Dan Pride was writing a book. He meant to end the
superstitition about Samuel and Elizabeth Pride. He
meant to show that troubles have come with the fog by
chance, and not because of the poor 'witches'. He often
sat just where you are sitting. Aye. We saw alike, Dan
Pride and I."

Dan felt that he had known Lamie all his life, and the
thought gave him courage. Eagerly he asked, "Did my
grandfather ever speak of a hiding place on Pride's Island?"

Lamie looked at him for a long moment. Dan read disappointment in the calm old face. "Aye. When he commenced to write his history he became much interested in
finding the witches' chamber—"

"Witches' chamber!" A thrill of excitement raised the
hair on Dan's neck. "At Pride's?"

"Aye. Somewhere at Pride's. Tradition says that such a
hideaway was built by the son of Samuel and Elizabeth.
But it was hidden well, since it was meant for members of
the household who might yet be accused of witchcraft."
Lamie shook his head in sorrow. "Fearful times were
those, when a man might not trust his neighbor, and one
evil led to another."

"But did my grandfather ever find this witches' chamber?"

"Aye. I think he did." The old man looked far out over the mist-haunted marsh, as if he were trying to see some distant face.

"Where?" Dan pressed him. "Where did he find it?"

But Lamie would not be hurried. "All one spring, he searched the old house until he commenced to doubt that there ever had been such a hiding place. There was no proof, you understand, only the legend. Then, one day, he discovered an early diary, and he learned that a hideaway had indeed been built. But not a word of its whereabouts."

Dan waited impatiently.

"Again he searched, in the house, and outside. But the months went by and he calculated that the chamber must have been destroyed, or else sealed up so perfectly that it would never be discovered until Pride's itself was torn down, beam from beam." Then Lamie smiled. "One day he seemed as excited as a boy, and I was glad for him. I guessed he had found at last what he had been seeking."

"But didn't he tell you about it?" Dan asked, disappointed.

Lamie shook his head. "I believe he meant to use the chamber as a secret place to store the family documents, which were priceless to him. He told me this, or perhaps I guessed it. It has been a long time."

Excitement ran like flame through Dan's veins. He was sure he knew what had happened. His grandfather had found the ancient witches' chamber! There, rather than in his office at Pride's, he had kept secure enough material to kill the old wives' tales for all time! Possibly the trusted Elder Corey, like Mrs. Corey herself, felt strongly against meddling in the past. So there in the forgotten chamber Daniel Pride had collected his proof against the Fiddler. There he had fled in his time of trouble. *And there,* thought Dan in triumph, *he had hidden the briefcase!*

"But didn't he ever hint where the room is?"

The hermit looked troubled, like a child. His tranquillity had gone. "No, nor did I ask. Later, after your good grandfather passed on, I heard that something was lost, something that would prove the Bishops dishonorable. It may have been this hiding place, or it may have been something Old Dan hid in this hiding place. I gather that the Prides spared no effort to find it, for revenge was in their hearts. But these were not good things to hear, and so I did not listen."

Lamie turned back to his beloved marsh, and peace returned to the old face. "There is no revenge out there. No hatred. Only the beauty: life, and the ending of life, and the beginning again."

Somewhere a night bird called. The river and the streams were returning to their beds, broad curves of silver in the bright night. The great flood tide was draining back, and the marsh belonged once more to the land.

"Lamie." Dan's voice was low in confession. "I hate the Bishops, too."

"Like your poor uncle, then," said the old man after a long moment. "Yet, I should have thought that you favored Dan Pride, your grandfather. I am seldom wrong about people."

Dan had to tell this simple man the whole truth. He said in a steady voice, "I hate them. It was a briefcase that was lost, with proof of their treachery. And I intend finding that briefcase and proving what the Bishops are really like! I'll prove what they've always been like, ever since they accused my ancestors of witchcraft!"

"Are these thoughts your own?" Lamie asked sadly.

"You mean, does Uncle Julian influence me? No. He never talks to me at all. He thinks he made a mistake to bring me to Prides!" Dan broke off hopelessly.

Lamie looked at him. Then he said, "You had better tell Lamie, from the beginning."

Then Dan told the old man about the orphaned years in England, and how he had hoped for a new home at Pride's Point. He told him how badly things had gone between him and his uncle from the time Dan had heard the Fiddler and talked of it aboard the *Three Sisters,* until they had read the name Philip Bishop on the lost knife. He tried to tell about his flight from the house tonight, but remorse and bitterness broke in his voice and he fell silent.

Lamie said softly, "Now you mean to prove your loyalty to your uncle—by seeking revenge against your friends."

"Friends!" Dan said tightly. "I'll find that briefcase if it's the last thing I ever do—"

"It is late," said Lamie. "Let us go back now."

The old man led the way down to the little cove and aboard the lobster boat. Dan helped cast off. He felt light-headed and at peace. He had gotten his fury off his chest;

he seemed to be moving through a dream that would end well.

With Caliban between them, they chugged out of the little harbor and around Lamie's Island to the point. Dan leaped ashore where the *Jinx* had struck, and tied the skiff on behind Lamie's work boat.

Then they headed up river against the tide. The moon was low. In the east the night began to pale. There was a rare sweetness in the air, and the birds were beginning to sing. It was beautiful beyond belief. Dan's throat filled strangely, and he remembered his first glimpse of the marsh, storm-swept and desolate. Lamie was right. He had, and without knowing it, come to love the salt marsh.

Just below the bridge, Lamie cut back the motor. Quietly they moved under the middle arch. A flock of mud-peeps lifted, wheeled, and returned to their feeding farther up the river. The new day had begun.

"We are here, my son," said Lamie at his side. "But this I must say before you go. Find what is lost and prove your loyalty to your uncle, if you can. But before you seek vengeance on your friends, ask yourself this: did they hide their family name to break the friendship between you? Or to keep it from breaking?"

Dan stared, heavy-eyed, at the hermit.

Lamie smiled. "Think about this after you have slept. And remember, Dan Pride. Sometimes you must judge your fellowmen by what they mean to do, rather than by what they do."

So saying, Lamie turned into the backwater, and

Caliban sprang ashore. Dan slipped into the skiff and cast off the tow line. "May I come again?" he called softly.

Lamie bowed with gentle ceremony. "Whenever you will." Without looking back, he moved out into the current and around the bend.

The boy pulled up the skiff and made it fast. He had talked with the hermit! He had been alone to his island; had ridden in his boat. And he had found that the people of York were wrong. Lamie was not crazy, but filled with wisdom and the love of good things.

In the thin dawn the old house looked forsaken. Noiselessly, Dan opened the heavy door. He was about to slip inside when Caliban pressed wishfully against him. Dan hesitated. He had supposed that after the night was over, the dog would return from force of habit to Billy Ben's cottage. He placed his hand warningly on the rough coat, and together the boy and the dog moved in silence up the stairs and into the room at the end of the dark hall. Very cautiously, without a sound, Dan closed his door. The night's adventure was over, and no one the wiser.

A few moments later in another part of the sleeping house, another door closed just as quietly.

CHAPTER FIFTEEN

A Bishop at Pride's

~~~~~~

EARLY in the morning Caliban whimpered at the door. When Dan let him out, Lamie's Island and its old master still were very close, more real than Dan's own room.

But when Dan rose groggily much later that morning, the night's adventure seemed like an improbable dream. And the witches' chamber. If it existed at all, why had Billy Ben not discovered it before? For surely it was this hiding room which he had been seeking for so long.

The day was overcast and the dark old house was chill. Billy Ben had lined up enough work in the gardens and hay barn to keep Dan busy for several hours. But as soon as he was free, Dan headed for the library.

Mrs. Corey had lighted the logs on the great hearth. But in this dark-paneled room with its grave portraits, the fire did little to lift Dan's spirits. Only discovering the witches' chamber could do that now, he thought grimly. For there would be the Pride papers!

He sat at a desk and began by mapping Pride's point.

After a painstaking hour, he had made a thorough sketch of the island and its buildings. But with the little he knew of the area, the map meant nothing. He needed local help desperately and there was no help. Not from his uncle, who wanted no part of him; nor from Lamie, who wanted no part of his revenge; nor ever again from the twins. He crushed the paper and hurled it into the fire.

How did one find a room hidden for three hundred years? Perhaps the past itself would help him. He searched among the heavy old books until he located one on superstition. Then he curled up near the fire, and the wind blew steady and raw across the marsh outside.

The Devil could come, he read, in the shape of a yellow bird, or a black dog, or a pig. A person who would possess magic powers had only to sign his name in the Devil's book to become, for all time, a witch. No one had questioned these things. The crime of witchcraft was recognized and punished by death.

When this very room was new, marveled Dan, good people actually believed such things. But had they ever truly stopped believing nonsense? For all over the world, people still persecuted the neighbor who was different from themselves. These were dark thoughts.

Suddenly a sharp rapping came at the window. Startled, Dan felt the blood flush into his face. It was Pip!

The boy's sandy head disappeared from the window and angry steps crossed the lawn. A hesitation at the door, then Pip stood before him.

"What do you mean, 'we set the fire and left you to take the blame'?" he demanded. It was as if he continued some hateful conversation which had unsettled his mind for a week.

Dan stared. "I don't know what you're talking about."

"Oh, you don't know what I'm talking about!"

"Keep your voice down," ordered Dan. His thoughts were in turmoil. *Here, in the library at Pride's Point, stood a Bishop!* Then came Lamie's words: "Did they hide their family name to break the friendship between you— or to keep it from breaking?"

For a moment Pip's voice lowered obediently. "Gilly says she's never going to speak to you again. And I even promised her I wouldn't come back here, at least yesterday. But this is today and now, by gosh, we're going to get things straightened out, Dan Pride!"

"Keep your voice down," snapped Dan. "Who said I blame you for the fire?"

"You mean you don't know what that baboon Billy Ben told me?" But there was doubt in Pip's voice.

"Go on."

"He said you think we set that fire, and then ran out on you. He said he tried to talk you out of it—" Pip stopped. There was no mistaking the bewildered look on Dan's face. He let out his breath. "The so-and-so lied!"

Dan nodded, wonderingly. It seemed that Billy Ben hoped to separate the friends, perhaps to prevent Dan from gaining help in his search.

The fury ebbed from Pip's face. "Well, it isn't the first time!" He thrust out his hand cheerfully. "Let's forget it, Dan. There's sure no reason for *us* to fight."

No reason. Again Dan saw the secret looks between Pip and Gilly. The hand stayed out between them. Resent-

ment rose like a flood, and Dan forgot Lamie's advice. He
turned his back and crossed to the window. "You know
how I feel about—the Bishops. *You* lied, you and Gilly.
You lied from the beginning!"

Behind him, Pip stood silent.

"Well, didn't you?"

Pip answered slowly, "We didn't mean to. We just—"

Dan waited coldly.

"I mean, it never made any difference to Gil and me who
your folks were. But we weren't sure you'd feel the same,
so we didn't say anything right off. Then you started to
hate our family and— Gosh, Dan, it just got harder and
harder to tell you—"

"That your mother was Ann Bishop, and your grandfather was Philip Bishop." Dan's voice was harsh.

"Well, we kept hoping you'd change your mind about
us. That's why we always cleared out before your uncle
came. We knew he wouldn't want any Bishops around
Pride's Point," he added practically.

As if in answer to his words, the straight figure of Dan's
uncle passed the library windows from the driveway.

"Quick," breathed Dan. "That way, into the office."

Without a question, Pip ducked into the room off the
library. Seconds later, Uncle Julian entered and closed the
door behind him. He saw Dan by the window, and mo-
tioned him to a chair.

"I'm glad you're here. I came home early to have a talk
with you." He sat down wearily.

Intent, Dan listened for any sound from the office, and
the silence grew heavy. Caliban whimpered from the hall

outside. Dan held his breath, but his uncle did not move to admit him.

"You have won the dog over completely," he said with a thin smile. "I saw you come up together from the marsh at dawn."

Dan stared. Was it possible that his uncle had worried last night? That he had stayed awake, perhaps, waiting for him to come home? The thought filled him with a joy which he quickly hid.

"You're the second friend Caliban has allowed himself. You should feel flattered, whatever happened last night." Uncle Julian was asking a question.

"I went to Lamie's," Dan said shortly.

His uncle leaned forward. "Why? If you please."

I was lonely. I wanted to run away, thought Dan. He looked at his feet. "My sunburn hurt and I went outside to cool off. I tried to be quiet."

"You were quiet," said his uncle dryly. "Go on."

Dan strained for any sound from Pip. Then he continued briefly, "Caliban was at the mooring. I thought he meant to go for me, and I got away in the skiff. But he followed, swimming. I was afraid he would drown so I pulled him into the boat. We came up against the point on Lamie's Island. Lamie brought us back."

Julian Pride studied his nephew for a long moment. "All that must have taken courage. Actually, the dog can swim as well as the muskrats he hunts. But you were wiser than you knew, since Caliban never forgets a kindness—or an injury."

Then his uncle mused, "Your grandfather was a great friend of the hermit. Lamie must be very old now."

"Then I may go again?" Dan asked eagerly.

Julian Pride shrugged. "Of course."

Dan felt a twinge of pity for him without understanding why.

"Another time, however, please arrange for Billy Ben to take you. It is not safe to row alone in that part of the marsh."

Dan said nothing. If he must go with Billy Ben, should he ever see the old hermit again?

"And don't believe everything Lamie has to say. He is a good man, but—simple. Not like other men."

The two fell silent. Uncle Julian rose and let the dog into the library. Caliban limped over to Dan and leaned against his knee. Then he tensed, raised his head toward the office. Desperate, Dan pushed the great body downward, and slowly Caliban obeyed. He stretched his deformed length between them and closed his eyes.

"He's a good dog," said Uncle Julian, "although Billy Ben is afraid he may turn vicious. He has wheedled me into restraining him most of the time." He studied the dog's thin flanks helplessly, as if Billy Ben had become too much for him.

Dan stared. "Then you don't think Caliban's a killer?"

His uncle laughed shortly. "Hardly. Although Billy Ben could be right, I suppose. The dog was—badly beaten once."

"But who—" Dan stopped, embarrassed.

"No, not I. Billy Ben. That surprises you? Well, people are the way they are," said his uncle heavily. "Billy Ben was afraid of the dog. He beat and maimed him one day several years ago, convinced that Caliban was trying to kill him."

Another silence. Then Julian Pride moved impatiently, as if he had other things to say. "I am sorry I judged you so harshly. But I should have preferred that you, rather than Mrs. Corey, had told me the truth: that you never knew your friends were—Bishops. That they, not you, were dishonest." He reached for a cigar.

The silence from the office now seemed heavier than the one which stretched between him and Uncle Julian. Then Dan said slowly, to Pip as well as to his uncle, "I don't think the twins meant to lie. I think they meant to keep our friendship going until I could—accept the fact they're Bishops." There. He had said the words which forgave Pip and Gilly for their secret. And silently, across the space of the two rooms, it seemed that Pip had again reached out his hand. This time Dan would have taken it.

"And now can you accept that fact?" The low voice was heavy with sarcasm. His uncle waited, lighting the cigar. And just beyond in his hiding place, waited the only friend Dan had ever had. Painfully, Dan debated within himself, and the minutes ticked past.

Finally his uncle said, "Years ago, your grandfather hoped to end the quarrel between the two families. I told you once of his plan to buy the shipyard from Philip Bishop."

Dan nodded, wondering which of the old troubles made his uncle's face go dark with emotion.

"Now let me tell you something I have never told another person, not even your father. I, too, had a plan, a purely personal one, that might have ended the feud in its own time. I hoped to marry Ann Bishop, you see. The trouble between our families meant little to either of us.

But because of it we met in secret, and we kept our plans secret. We intended to announce them as soon as our fathers had completed their business." Julian Pride's voice went on mechanically. He seemed to have forgotten that Dan was in the room.

"In a way, the sale of the shipyard was a symbol. If it succeeded, then Prides and Bishops could consider the feud a thing of the past." Uncle Julian studied the sleeping animal at his feet. "As you know, it did not succeed." He hesitated. "What nobody knows is that your grandfather carried to the meeting that night a briefcase filled with currency, not securities at all. Cash."

Dan listened, not really understanding.

"This is not the usual practice, of course. But all you need to know is that it was a token of good faith between two old enemies. And it was Ann Bishop's idea."

Dan went cold, as if a sharp wind had blown against his perspiring skin.

"I myself proposed it to my father. It was exactly the sort of idea he appreciated. I'm certain that he delivered the cash in good faith to the Bishops and received the papers to prove it. I am certain, too, that some hireling of Philip Bishop then followed him home and robbed him of the papers . . . a monstrous act of faithlessness!" his uncle added, roughly. "Hard, hard to accept."

Dan nodded, seeing all too clearly what must have happened: a change of heart on Philip Bishop's part, and Ann's love less strong than the hatreds of the old feud.

"I fought against believing. But the facts themselves proved Philip Bishop guilty. As Elder Corey argued—and he was to be trusted—it was not a matter of highway robbery by some stranger. Only the two families knew of the cash in the first place, and the Pride household certainly could be ruled out."

"But what about Ann Bishop?" Dan asked. "Perhaps she didn't even know."

His uncle shrugged. "Blood is thicker than water." He was silent for a long moment. Then he added, "And Philip Bishop had a motive. Those were lean years in the shipyard business. By this move he would lose nothing, neither the price, nor the property. And without any trace of the briefcase, there was not the slightest evidence against him."

Viciously, Uncle Julian cast his cigar into the hearth. "Once again it was another case of Bishops betraying Prides! It was this that really killed my father, I think." He stared blindly into the fire. "That next morning, I was the one who found him."

The silence, heavy with years and tragedy, lengthened between them and reached into the office. The dining room clock whirred, and struck three, echoed by the case clock on the landing. In his mind, Dan saw Pip's hand withdrawn for all time. The boy had heard his mother accused of treachery. No friendship could survive this, Dan thought dully.

His uncle continued. "Once Ann Bishop sent a note asking to meet me at the bridge. But I did not go. I couldn't have seen her again, whatever her excuses, after what had happened. Perhaps she came—I never knew."

Julian Pride stared down at his hands. "In time, she left town and married. Later, when her children were still small, she lost her husband and returned to York. I have not seen her since she left, except at a distance. I have never met her children, and do not wish to. Now I think you will understand when I say you are not to see them again, for any reason. And if you meet them by chance, you will have nothing to do with them."

Uncle Julian rose tiredly and went to the window. He has something left to say that is even more difficult, thought Dan with a sinking heart. The broad marsh lay rain-swept and desolate beyond.

"In the fall you had better plan to go away to school again, away from the Bishops."

Dan stared, shocked into silence.

"And away from me. I have been a poor substitute for a family, I'm afraid."

"No!" cried Dan. "No!"

Uncle Julian shook his head. "I know nothing about young people. You haven't been happy here."

Dan protested, but Uncle Julian went firmly on. "Furthermore, according to Billy Ben there is talk in town. More of the old gossip, and this time it involves you." His uncle added in a hard voice, "We can do without this. There are better places for you than Pride's Point."

Dan gripped the edge of his chair. His throat filled, and he could not say the words that cried to be said.

His uncle looked at him kindly. But the sunken eyes were already remote, as if by retreating into his other world he might keep the troubles of this one at a distance. "No. It was a mistake to bring you here. And perhaps they're right. Perhaps Pride's is a place with a curse on it, and should be gotten rid of—"

A sudden clatter from the office sent Dan's heart against

his chest. Julian Pride gave an exclamation. He strode across the room and flung open the door. The window gaped wide, but Dan saw with relief that the room was empty. The drapes were flapping in the wind and papers blew about the desk. Caliban sniffed at the sill.

Irritably, Uncle Julian closed and locked the window. "Mrs. Corey is growing careless, particularly when the weather is bad." Resigned, he sat down at his desk to sort his papers.

Dan wanted desperately to talk—about staying at Pride's; about his determination to find the briefcase; about Lamie, and the witches' chamber. He needed to tell Uncle Julian about Billy Ben's search, and about Pip's visit. Most of all he had to make his uncle understand his loyalty. Instead he stood there, dumb and miserable.

"Thank you, Dan," said Uncle Julian without looking up. It was dismissal, stripped of feeling.

Dan turned and went out.

As he passed the dining room, he saw Samuel's black eyes upon him. Revenge? Was this the message? Lamie would say no, in spite of the bitter story of Ann Bishop's treachery.

What, then, if not revenge? The eyes blazed into his. Dan looked uneasily away and moved on. Perhaps time would tell.

CHAPTER SIXTEEN

Treasure Hidden, Treasure Lost

~~~~~~

DURING the next few rainy days Dan thought often of the talk with Uncle Julian. At last he knew the full reason for his uncle's malice, and Dan was filled with pity. But worse, he knew that after Ann Bishop's betrayal any friendship between the two families was surely doomed.

On the other hand he yearned to see Pip again, and tell him that he understood. Lamie was right. The twins had kept their identity secret because they intended good, not harm. Now Pip would not come back to Pride's Point. And Dan was to have nothing more to do with the twins.

Bitterly, Dan kept busy in order to forget the turmoil in his mind.

Work outdoors was impossible during this bad weather. So with the rain pelting against the windows, Billy Ben found odd jobs for Dan and himself to do inside. Dan did his share in the house and barns without complaint. And

Billy Ben kept a hawk's eye on him, constant, calculating.

Still, whenever Dan could get clear of the hired man, he explored the old house and its buildings with a vengeance. The witches' chamber was constantly in his mind. Now he saw it sealed behind a wall; and he sounded bricks and panels for the echo which would give away its hiding place. Next, its entrance was cunningly concealed in a dirt floor. Then, alone, he prowled the creepy fastnesses of the old cellars, his eyes wide and sharp.

Shortly before lunch one day he was sent to the attic to replenish Billy Ben's stock of paint cloths. He was about to descend with the rag bag, when he noticed a dark opening low in the eaves. With a racing heart, he crawled through. There, at a lower level, was a second attic, sparred by giant rafters and dimly lit by a skylight. He knew from the roof's steep pitch that he stood in the loft of Samuel Pride's original dwelling!

He forgot his errand. Bemused, he tapped the walls, examined the gables, the worn floor. At last he rose, stiff and disappointed. There was no room, however small, hidden in the old loft. He crawled back to the main attic.

A figure was leaning lazily against a beam. Dan felt the color leave his cheeks. But Billy Ben only smiled broadly, turned, and went down the narrow stairs to lunch.

He knows! Dan told himself. *He's wondered for several days, and now he knows!* For in the same instant, Dan remembered the door to the chapel. He had left it yawning wide the night he went there alone. There would no longer be any safety in pretending friendship. From now on, he must be careful.

And about at this time, apparently Uncle Julian insisted on Caliban's freedom. For each morning the dog came to Dan and remained faithfully beside him. Otherwise, Dan was sure, Billy Ben would have sought him out. Somehow the man would have pried out of him Lamie's story that old Dan had discovered the witches' chamber. Somehow he would have ferreted out the secret of the fortune still in the briefcase. So the boy was grateful for the dog's companionship. There was no question about it: Billy Ben was mortally afraid of Caliban, and the dog sensed it. He bristled at the hired man's approach and eyed him with hostility. If Caliban ever lets loose, Dan told himself anxiously, I'll not be able to control him!

But the gray days passed and nothing further happened. Billy Ben kept his distance. Pride's Point held fast to its ancient secret, and Dan began to feel a deep urgency. Summer was going swiftly now. Soon fall would come, and with it another change, another strange place. If he were to locate the lost chamber and vindicate the wrong done to his family, he must act fast.

One morning, on impulse, Dan asked Uncle Julian to drop him off at the library in York. There he read through a wealth of material on colonial customs and architecture, hungry for any mention of hideouts built in the houses of the first planters.

Pride's had much in common, he learned, with other dwellings of the period: its several gables; its steep-pitched roofs; its lean-to, long and dark; its great garrets and uneven cellars; its facing south as accurately as a compass. One photograph of an ancient homestead showed a staircase built inside a vast chimney as a means of escape during the witchcraft terror. This last bit of information came excitingly close to the story of Pride's Point, but it still did not give him the answer he sought. Finally Dan looked up and gazed through the window at the busy life of the town. How could he go about locating a hiding place built—and hidden well—at Pride's Point so long ago?

"Is there a museum in town where I might find some of the Pride records, or possibly a plan of the old house?" Dan asked the librarian.

She smiled. "Your nice Billy Ben Corey asked that same question some time ago," she said. "But even our York Museum has few records of the old Pride place. We think your grandfather collected such things years ago when he was preparing his book." She was very sorry. Perhaps if Dan were to search the house itself, he would find the papers he wanted. She urged him warmly to come again, and Dan left with the feeling that it could be good to live in a small town where people knew you.

On his way out he held the door for a woman with two small boys. He was feeling friendly, he was not on his guard. So what happened next came as a shock. The older boy stared hard at Dan, and whispered to his brother, "It's that Dan Pride. You ketch his eye, you're hexed!"

The smaller boy glanced wildly up at Dan. Then his eyes darted away in panic. The woman hushed both boys sharply, and the heavy door closed.

His cheeks flaming, Dan walked out into the fine mist. He made his way past the monument and on down Main

Street. As before, he walked the several miles home across the East Marsh with his pride sick inside him.

He was a jinx. To children, as well as to certain grown-ups, his name meant trouble. Desperately Dan cast about in his mind. He had to talk this over with someone his own age! Pip and Gilly Cole. The children of Ann Bishop. He seemed to hear his uncle's voice, cold, bitter: "You will have nothing to do with them." For the first time, Dan debated whether to ignore his uncle's order. He could cross the bridge this very day to the Bishop place!

But then he reached Pride's. Weary and wet, he whistled to Caliban instead. Together they took refuge in the library until Billy Ben came looking for him to get on with some painting in the carriage house.

Before the day was over, Dan was glad that he had not broken faith with his uncle. For Uncle Julian arrived home early that afternoon. The dark set of his face had somehow altered. It was replaced by a look of pleasure which was hurtingly familiar to Dan, half-forgotten.

"Come out to the car, Dan. I've got something for you." It was his father's look, his father's voice. Dan's heart gave a lurch. In a few weeks even this would be taken away. But with Caliban between them, he went with his uncle to the carriage house. There in the trunk of the car was an outboard motor, small, but sleek and new.

"Now you can explore the marsh more easily and safely. And visit Lamie when you like," Uncle Julian added.

It took all Dan's self-control to hide his emotion. For a painful sense of the loss to come, rushed in and mingled with the gratitude. He spoke his thanks briefly. Then, without talking, they went down to the mooring rock.

Here, feeling closer to his uncle than ever before, Dan learned how to operate the outboard motor. Under the pewter sky they went up and down the river, first with Uncle Julian, then Dan, at the helm. And when his uncle left Dan sensed in him a new feeling, a puzzled warmth, as if the man had at last bridged some gap between himself and the boy, only to find the door barred.

Now the thought of leaving Pride's and his uncle had become an intolerable ache. Dan could bear it only by pretending indifference to Uncle Julian, and to himself.

Hopefully Caliban climbed into the skiff and sat down. Dan decided on the spot to go to Lamie's Island. As they moved away from the mooring rock, he heard the sound of a spade. Clearly Billy Ben was taking advantage of the fact that the rain, at last, had stopped. With an effort, Dan closed his mind for the moment on Billy Ben and his long search for the witches' chamber.

They nosed into the half-tide, heading eastward under the bridge. The little motor beat hard against the current. River and sky alike were dull gray, as if the sun itself had forsaken the earth. The waterways lay like glass. It had been like this, Dan remembered, before the last heavy fog. But that, too, he could worry about later.

With a feeling of freedom, he wound his way through the vast salt meadows. Gradually the old roofs and gables of Pride's, the great beeches, disappeared behind the thrust of the islands in the East Marsh. Well below the Gut, Dan eased the skiff into the little cove at Lamie's Island and up to the dock. His first landing!

As before, the old hermit met them with a courtly bow.

"Welcome. Welcome," he said. "Come up to the house, please."

They followed him up the steep path to the driftwood cottage, and Caliban settled contentedly on the grass outside to wait. Dan gazed about with delight as Lamie stirred a pot on his little cook stove. The cottage smelled of hot chocolate, and of spruce and the sea. The four walls were lined with worn books, and there was a table with two chairs like the two outside under the thorn tree. Beside the neat cot was a sea chest covered with everyday objects. A battery-powered radio, an ice box scoured clean of its paint, and an orderly cupboard—these completed the furnishings. It was cozy and homelike. Somehow familiar. Dan glanced back at the sea chest, and his heart leaped into his throat. There, among the old man's few belongings, was the rusty black shape of a violin case!

Lamie followed his gaze. He said gently, "Yes, my boy. The violin is my most prized possession. It was the gift of your grandfather."

Dan's voice faltered, but he forced himself to ask the question: "Could your violin be heard as far away as Pride's?"

Lamie smiled sadly. "You ask yourself if those who hear the music near the old bridge, hear only Lamie playing his violin. No, my son. That is too simple an answer for those who believe in a Fiddler. In any case, Lamie's Island is too far away.—Now drink this, and tell Lamie what has brought you."

Dan finished the drink, which was hot and rich. Then he told Lamie about Pip's visit to Pride's. Lamie nodded, but said nothing. Dan told about the talk with his uncle.

He told how Pip, hiding in the office, had heard Julian Pride's ugly story about Ann Bishop.

"Aye," said Lamie softly. "To love someone, then to believe this one has turned against you—that is a cupful of hemlock. And for the boy to hear this of his mother— that is another cupful."

Then flatly and without feeling, Dan told Lamie about his uncle's order that he was not to see the twins again. "He thinks I must leave Pride's in the fall," said Dan evenly, "and go to school somewhere away from York."

Lamie got to his feet and opened his door. "Listen, my son."

Dan heard the sharp whistle of a grackle overhead. Then, faintly, came an answering cry from the island shore as if the birds were in conversation.

"Everything seeks out its own kind," said Lamie in his slow way, as if this were the answer.

But Dan was still puzzled.

"Go to see your friend now that you need him, just as he came to you. Only tell your uncle that you have gone. He, too, needs a friend. And perhaps, if you have courage, perhaps that friend will be you."

Dan shook his head doubtfully.

Lamie said, "Once there lived a saint, a holy man of Assisi. He was a simple man, known for his love of nature and of men. He, too, knew the peace of the rivers and the channels. He said wise things. Would you like to hear them?"

Dan nodded.

The ancient man closed his eyes and leaned his head back against the chair. Then he quoted softly, " 'Lord, make me a channel of thy peace, that where there is hatred I may bring love. Where there is wrong, I may bring the spirit of forgiveness. Where there is error, I may bring truth—' "

The grackles rejoiced in the trees. The afternoon sang with their joy.

Not hatred, but love, thought Dan. Not revenge, but forgiveness. Not lies, but truth. Truth. *The truth about the Bishops!*

"I've searched everywhere at Pride's," he said in answer. "The house, the barns, the carriage house. But there's not a trace of the witches' chamber. I'm beginning to think it must be somewhere outside!"

Sadly, Lamie shook his head. "You are searching for the briefcase, for proof against your neighbor. Yet I think you do not hate your friends. Why, then, do you still seek revenge on them?"

Dan stared at the old man. It was a good question. He wanted more than ever to find the briefcase. But some strange alchemy had taken place in his reason for finding it. He said slowly, "Uncle Julian is eaten up with hatred. He's certain that Ann Bishop and her family betrayed him. The briefcase will prove whether he's wrong, I know it will. I've got to find it now, for his sake, and Pip's, and mine." His voice rose eagerly. "Supposing the Bishops didn't lie! If they weren't guilty of the attack on my grandfather, then someone else was!"

Old Lamie looked bewildered. "Attack? The Bishops guilty of attack?"

"Uncle Julian thinks that my grandfather completed his business at the Bishops' house, and later that night someone hired by Philip Bishop followed him home and robbed him of the proof," Dan explained. "But the Bishops claim my grandfather never reached their house at all! They said they never received any money and never made any sale. Uncle Julian is sure they lied."

Lamie shook his head pleasantly. "No, they did not lie. Your good grandfather never even crossed the bridge that night. So he could not have reached the Bishop house, you see."

Dan felt dizzy, as if he stood at the edge of a great drop.

"It is true, and I will tell you how I know," said Lamie simply. "I was fishing that night at the ebb of the tide. I was just below the old bridge, listening, and looking, and smelling the good smells of the fog and the night." He paused, remembering.

"And then I saw the lights, the strange lights such as they talk about. One light was the electric lantern which your grandfather carried as he came down through the willows with his briefcase."

"Yes. Yes," said Dan, unaware that he had spoken.

"The fog was very thick, and so I saw him only dimly. I did not call out lest I frighten the heron which was fishing on the flats. I saw his light reach the bridge, even though the fog had shut him out. His light made a very pretty rainbow circle in the mist, I remember."

Dan nodded, scarcely breathing. That night of terror was coming to life before his eyes.

Lamie squinted in concentration. "Behind his light came another, a strange light. It came fleet and soft, like an Indian, from tree to tree. Then the second light drew

near the first. There was a blurring of lights, and then the
good darkness again. I heard running, not over the
bridge toward the Bishops', but out into the old West
Marsh where it is not safe to go on foot at night. Once I
thought I heard a shout. Then one came stumbling back
toward the causeway road. Then there was nothing."

The old hermit fell silent for so long that Dan thought
he had finished. Then he spoke again. "Soon the other
came, fleet and soft, hunting with his light like a poacher
jacking deer. Up he went through the willows, and then
there was nothing more. Nothing more except a bad feeling. The night's white beauty was all spoiled and broken.
I waited a long time for it to come back. Then I rowed
home against the tide." Lamie sighed, and came back to
the present. "You see, my son, your good grandfather did
not go over the bridge to the Bishops' that night."

A din of bells was clamoring inside Dan's head. *The
Bishops had not lied!* Dan Pride had never reached their
house! He had started out with a fortune in currency. He
had been attacked, and he had escaped into the West
Marsh, with his briefcase. Mrs. Corey had said that the
marks in the mud proved this. Then he had stumbled back
toward Pride's Island and had somehow disappeared before he reached the causeway! Next his pursuer had
come searching for him, had finally, perhaps, left Pride's
Island over the east causeway in the fog. And later, later,
they had found Dan Pride, fallen, without his briefcase,
his treasure hidden—or lost.

"Lamie," said Dan in a hoarse voice, "I have to go
now."

"Go, you and your caged-up troubles," smiled Lamie.

"But soon let your troubles go free like wild, dark birds. Then you will return to Lamie in peace."

Dan raced down the path to the rickety wharf. He fairly leaped into the skiff with Caliban at his heels. Above, the grackles scattered in flight, and the herring gulls rose screaming into the slate gray sky.

CHAPTER SEVENTEEN

By Fair Means or Foul

WITH the excitement common to all bearers of great news, Dan took the north branch of the river to the Bishops'. He had uncovered facts which would set both families by the ears! At its best speed the skiff seemed scarcely to be moving.

But finally he rounded the last bend and saw Pip and Gilly like a still life painting, fishing from their float. They watched his approach in silence, with no sign of welcome.

Dan cut the motor and nosed alongside the float. Without a word, Pip caught the painter and knotted it deftly around a cleat. Gilly looked up river, as mute as a stone. Clearly, neither of the twins meant to ask him ashore, so Dan stayed where he was, holding the *Jinx* steady against the float.

The water lapped at the hull. A green-head fly buzzed angrily about their heads, then lost itself in the marsh. As Dan groped for the proper words, the memory of Uncle

Julian's voice filled the silence, low and tense: *You are not to see these children again, for any reason!*

Pip looked uncomfortable, as if he wished he were elsewhere. "Well, what are *you* doing here?" he asked.

"I've been to Lamie's," said Dan simply.

"Lamie's!" Gilly glanced at him with respect, then looked swiftly away.

"Alone again?" asked Pip wistfully, and Dan nodded. Pip, hidden in the office at Pride's, had already heard Dan's story of his first visit to Lamie's Island.

"He told me something you both ought to hear," said Dan.

Pip waited willingly enough. But Gilly flopped onto her stomach and stared sullenly at the incoming tide.

"I don't know how to say this." Dan drew a deep breath as truth struggled with family pride. "But—my uncle is wrong. My family was always dead certain that my grandfather bought the shipyard from your grandfather. And they swore your family lied when they claimed he hadn't."

The twins waited in cold silence.

"Well, your family didn't lie. My grandfather never reached your house that night. He never got farther than the bridge."

Pip's blue eyes remained on his, bright now and interested. But Gilly frowned, avoiding his look.

"Your mother had nothing to do with the—trouble."

"We know," said Pip. "But who did?"

The entire marsh seemed to be holding its breath, waiting for Dan's answer.

"Someone who knew my grandfather was carrying a

great lot of money. Lamie was out fishing. He saw the whole thing."

"Who? Who was it?" Pip's calm voice was loud with impatience. Gilly turned, her eyes wide on Dan.

Dan shook his head helplessly. "Lamie couldn't tell. It was night time, you see—"

Pip nodded. "And a Fiddler's fog."

"Lamie saw my grandfather's light," continued Dan, "as he came from Pride's to the bridge. Then a second light followed his, and the lights came together. Then Lamie heard running in the West Marsh, then someone stumbling back toward the causeway—and nothing else. After a while, he saw someone run back toward Pride's, shining his light, hunting my grandfather down. But whoever it was didn't find him. Nobody found him—until the next morning. That's all." Dan stopped wearily. There was something, something here which he should remember . . .

"Dan. Come on up and sit down," Pip said suddenly. The two boys glanced at each other, and understanding was warm between them.

Dan stepped onto the float. But as Caliban prepared to follow, the boy caught Gilly's look of alarm. "Stay," he ordered, and the dog sank back and rested his ugly head patiently on his paws.

"They say that dog'll tear you apart if he gets the chance. How come *you* ever—" Pip stopped in confusion.

Dan smiled thinly, remembering how timid he must seem. "I expect it's Billy Ben who started that story. He hates Caliban, and the feeling is mutual."

Pip eyed the dog with awe. "He's all yours. He'd scare the feathers off a crow."

"I'd rather have a cobra for a pet," Gilly said coldly.

Pip winked at Dan. "Tell us about Lamie," he urged.

Dan tried to describe the old man and his island. He told them of his first trip to Lamie's that moonlit night when he met Caliban at the mooring rock. He told them of the lost witches' chamber where old Dan must have kept his papers and later hidden his briefcase. "It was built as a hiding place in case—anyone accused others in our family of witchcraft."

Gilly took this personally and struck like a cat. "Lamie's crazy! Witches' chamber, my hat! And those lights he told about don't prove a thing, except maybe that awful story about the Fiddler paying back old Mr. Pride for laughing at the curse!"

The three sat silently, and the tide rippled and rose.

Then Pip said matter-of-factly, "So it's the Fiddler again. Then why didn't he just spirit away the briefcase, if he just meant to punish Old Dan? But the marks in the marsh showed that old Mr. Pride got away with the case from whoever was chasing him. So what Lamie's story really proves is that someone—a live person, not a ghost—actually followed Old Dan that night!"

"And from Pride's Point, not from here," Dan pointed out. "Running quick and light, like an Indian," he added thoughtfully.

"Well, it certainly wasn't anyone from our house," snapped Gilly, spoiling for battle. "And I should hope it wasn't your uncle, or your own father. That leaves Lamie, doesn't it? Or the Fiddler. Take your pick."

"Why don't you go up home till you feel better, Gil?" said Pip. "You're acting like a cussed girl."

"Horrid, isn't she?" grinned Dan. But he felt bereft,

confused. If only Gilly would be his friend again. And if only she could know the gentle old man who lived alone on his island in the East Marsh. Dan had a warm vision of the little driftwood house, and of Lamie with his eyes closed, remembering.

The east wind stirred, and bore the first low moaning of the fog horn. But Dan did not hear it. For a thought had sprung, black and enormous, from the back of his mind.

"Lamie said the footsteps that followed my grandfather were fast, and light. Billy Ben walks fast and light. Mrs. Corey once said that Billy Ben walks *exactly the way his father did—*"

Pip stared. Then he shook his head. "Elder Corey was liked and trusted. Everyone always said so."

Dan corrected him. "Everyone but Lamie. Lamie sees things for himself."

"Huh," said Gilly, hatefully.

"Lamie said my grandfather was a man without pretense, but that Elder Corey was not. He said my grandfather had put Elder Corey in charge of his affairs at Pride's."

Now, without being aware of it, they had begun to speak softly.

"Then Elder Corey could have known of the money!" Pip declared.

Dan nodded. "Uncle Julian said that no one knew, except himself and my grandfather and Ann Bishop—I mean your mother. But I expect he simply took Elder Corey for granted."

Pip mused, "Billy Ben's father could have followed Old Dan and attacked him. Maybe he hadn't planned it. Maybe the Fiddler's fog gave him the idea. Anyway, Old

Dan got away from him in the marsh and hid the briefcase. Then he had his heart attack after it was over."

Gilly's eyes were round. "Do you suppose Billy Ben
knows about the money?"

The boys stared at Gilly as the truth exploded before
them.

Dan's pulse pounded in his temples. "That's it! *The
money!* Billy Ben came to work at Pride's right after his
father died. Elder Corey must have told him there's a
fortune in that briefcase, and that it never left the island!
Because ever since Billy Ben came, he's been searching
for something!"

"You sure?" asked Pip with awe.

Dan nodded. "First the house, Mrs. Corey told me. Now
he's turning the island itself upside down. He pretends to
be working on projects of his own, like digging drains and
repairing foundations, but that's rot, of course! I guessed
some time ago that he's searching for the briefcase. But it
isn't Pride papers he wants, it's the money!"

Pip jumped to his feet, and the float rocked on the tide.
"Then we'll have to beat him to it! Because if Billy Ben
finds the briefcase first, he'll just empty it and leave it
laying around somewhere."

"Lying around," said Gilly automatically, forgetting her
anger for a moment. "Your uncle already thinks my family's guilty. So an empty briefcase would prove it for
sure—"

"And the feud will go on," Dan said slowly.

Something was bothering Pip. Finally he blurted,
"What if we do find it first? And what if there's a receipt
in it, but no money? That would prove your grandfather

did buy the shipyard, wouldn't it? And my own family lied."

"That's the craziest thing I ever heard!" declared Gilly in a fury. "And you can do your own hunting. Count me out!"

Disappointed, Dan turned away from Gilly's flushed face. "You too, Pip?"

Pip returned his look steadily. "I'm with you. We'll find the thing if it's there. And it'll have the money in it. It's got to!" Deliberately, he reeled in his line.

Again the sense of haste gripped Dan. He even found himself speaking swiftly. "Billy Ben must have ruled out the other hiding places, one by one. Now, I think, he's settled on the chapel." And Dan told them about the man's fury when he had tried to help at the foundation. "That was when I found out he hated me. Possibly he's always hated me, ever since I came."

"Probably. With what he has in mind, he sure can do without a kid snooping around. 'Specially three kids." Pip grinned in his old, easy fashion. "No wonder he told us that whopper. Anything to split up the three of us."

Dan was looking at Gilly. "Apparently he succeeded."

"I'd keep my eyes open if I were you, Dan," added Pip gravely. "Billy Ben would like to see you leave Pride's, I'll bet. He might even help you leave,—by fair means or foul."

Gilly sniffed in disbelief.

"If there's any time the three of us ought to stick together, Gil, it's now," snapped her brother. "We ought to get over there and sneak a look at what Billy Ben's up to, and figure out some way to beat him at his own game!"

But Gilly stared grimly toward Pride's Island and re-fused to answer.

She's thinking of what Uncle Julian said about her mother, thought Dan miserably. And she blames me, since I'm a Pride.

Pip threw a disgusted look at his sister. "Looks like it's up to us, Dan. Let's get rolling."

They left Gilly hunched on the float alone. Dan gazed back helplessly until they rounded the bend.

"There's been a big fog bank off the coast all day," Pip announced. "You can see it real clear from the house."

"A pity it isn't rolling in right now," said Dan. "Then we should be hidden in case someone is looking this way from Pride's."

"Billy Ben?"

"Uncle Julian, too," Dan said heavily. "If we're found together, Pip, that would be the end of things between my uncle and me."

Pip studied the banks above them, thick with thatch. "The tide's still low enough, don't worry. No one can see us from Pride's."

But Dan felt uneasy, oppressed. He cut the motor just above the Gut. The skiff drifted silently upstream toward Pride's Island. Now and then he gave a turn of the oar to guide their passage between the banks and under the bridge. His very movements felt heavy. He had a sense of grim developments just ahead—dark endings to events begun in years long gone. The charm's wound up, he thought. Now what would happen would happen. He could prevent it no more than he could stop the fog from creeping in over the land tonight.

Above them loomed the mooring rock. Clumsily, Caliban leaped ashore. He sniffed around the cave-in, hopeful of starting up a muskrat or an otter.

The boys were careful to make no sound as they pulled the *Jinx* onto its mooring. The harsh sounds of the spade continued, methodical, slower now that the afternoon was ending.

Suddenly alarmed, Dan whispered, "Where's Caliban?"

Pip scanned the causeway. "He won't give us away, will he?"

"He wouldn't mean to." Dan whistled softly. Caliban did not come. The dog was nowhere to be seen on the bridge or on the causeway.

"Maybe he cut through the woods," said Pip.

Dan groaned. "If he did, then Billy Ben will soon be looking for me. That's where the chapel is."

Pip understood in a flash. "I better get out of here." He scrambled up the causeway, heading for the bridge and the shadows of Oak Island.

"Wait," breathed Dan. "There he is!"

Caliban was swimming in the backwater below, as serene and sleek as an otter himself. He clambered up the bank and shook himself.

"Let's get going," whispered Pip, relieved. "We can sneak up through the woods, can't we? and come out behind the chapel, and see just what Billy Ben—" He paused. "What's wrong?"

Dan said slowly, "We ought to have heard Caliban when he jumped in—"

"Well, we didn't. What's so queer about that?"

Dan shook his head. "I don't know." Then he whispered, "I do know, Pip! He went down into the cave-in! He must have gone *through the causeway*, and out at the backwater!"

"Sure thing," said Pip, not understanding.

"Pip! Causeways are solid, aren't they? But not this one! There's a way *through* this one! That old stonework—Do you think—?"

Pip's mouth dropped. "By gosh. You think that's the witches' chamber down in there?"

Dan's voice rose in triumph. "No, but I'll bet it leads to it!"

The boys scrambled over the tossed rocks and peered down. Below them the stonework lay dim and mystifying, keeping its ancient secret to itself.

Dan leaped down to the mooring rock and, crouching, studied the faint symbol beneath.

"The double triangle. It was their roadmark, Pip. They used it to mark the ancient highway to Boston. And to those who knew, it also marked the way to—some sort of passage down here inside the causeway! Possibly a sort of escape tunnel from the witches' chamber, leading to the sea!"

Pip took this in. Then he pointed excitedly. "Maybe they even planned the mooring rock to stick out this way to hide the entrance—if there is one down there under the river!" He leaned far over. Then he said in disgust. "You can't tell. Tide's too high."

Dan drew a quick breath. "Mrs. Corey told me once that Samuel's son Hugh repaired this causeway soon after the witch trials. But they didn't need the old highway anymore. Everyone was already using the new road across the East Marsh. Pip, *he was building an escape tunnel here*, in case they accused other members of the family! And he kept it secret from the town!"

"Secret is right," said Pip, peering into the backwater, quiet and deep below. "It isn't just the mooring rock that hides the entrance. Every tide hides it too, from mid-tide up. If there's a passage down under here, then it's free just at low tide. What good's that?"

"I think I understand," said Dan in a hushed voice. "A passage here would provide an escape to the sea. And at low tide, the marsh itself would hide a small boat making for the coast."

"By gosh!" Pip's eyes were shining.

"And look! This causeway lies in a direct line with the chapel. The escape tunnel must once have run underground from the chapel all the way to the river!"

"Maybe it still does!" Pip put in.

"Then the hideout has to be in the chapel!" continued Dan with mounting excitement. "An accused witch could stay there for some time if he had to. He could go in for a last prayer—and disappear. His enemies would say witchcraft, of course!"

With their eyes, the boys traced a line from the grove which hid the chapel, down to the gray water. As they did, the dark and violent past came to life.

"And when it came low water," cried Pip, "he'd follow the passage to the river, and head for the coast. I bet they even kept a boat handy, maybe tied up to that old spike we use!"

Dan nodded. He forgot the need for caution and his voice rang clear. "It's exactly what I should have done if

I'd been Hugh Pride and seen both my parents jailed for witchcraft!" Then he added, "There's only one thing wrong. There's nothing inside the chapel. It's like a stone coffin—no closets, no cellar, nothing. There's no place for a hideout anywhere inside at all."

"Inside," repeated Pip. "Then if it isn't inside the chapel, the chamber's under it. It's got to be!"

Both boys grew meditative.

"Dan," said Pip suddenly, "if there is a hideout up there, Billy Ben may uncover it anytime. Tomorrow, even. Then, what?"

"Then we can't wait till tomorrow," said Dan slowly. "We'll come back at low water tonight. We'll try for it through the passage, from this spot."

"Tide won't be dead low till after ten," said Pip impatiently.

Dan stared hard at the cave-in, at the river. "Then let's meet here at nine. If we don't mind a wetting, possibly we can get in before low water."

"We'll get in all right, if there's still a way in," said Pip with enthusiasm. "We'll follow the passage all the way up to the hideout. We'll see for ourselves if that's where Old Dan hid the briefcase!"

"I'm sure of it!" cried Dan. "Lamie lost sight of my grandfather's light just here, at the causeway."

Pip nodded eagerly. "And the tide was low that night, so he could have—"

Caliban growled, a deep, controlled, primitive warning. The boys whirled around.

On the causeway above stood Billy Ben. A strange excitement glowed in the round blue eyes. With dismay Dan knew that he had heard enough to return here at low tide and search the causeway for himself. But first, by one means or another, he would have to get rid of both boys.

"Danny Boy," said Billy Ben with heavy concern. "Doesn't your word of honor mean anything at all?"

Dan's heart started a wild drumbeat.

Billy Ben said softly to Pip, "I thought I told you to keep away from here." He turned back to Dan. "Looks like you've broke your solemn promise to your uncle."

He took a quick step downward toward the boys. Caliban growled again, and Billy Ben stayed where he was. "Well, you want me to forget I saw you two together? Forget you're a liar, Danny Boy?"

Dan opened his mouth to defend himself. He would tell the good reasons for breaking his word to his uncle. He would shout that he knew all about Billy Ben's projects, all about the money, that he was not to be fooled any longer, not to be treated like a child!

But then he remembered Samuel. The old Puritan's silence during his long ordeal. The dark eyes luminous, piercing into his own. Suddenly he understood. The message was not *Revenge!* It was *Silence! Silence!* when speech meant danger.

Dan stared back into eyes that were round and hard as agates. He bit his underlip until the blood came, salty on his tongue. Softly Billy Ben taunted him.

"Scared to speak up, Danny Boy?" The man shook his head regretfully. "But I wouldn't be loyal to your Uncle Julian if I didn't report this, now would I?"

Dan swallowed repeatedly. He seemed to be drowning in his own saliva.

Billy Ben shrugged. "He won't feel much like trusting you outside your room for a while. Of course, I'll do what I can." He smiled broadly. "To help, I mean."

Double talk. Billy Ben seemed to be only an understanding, deeply disappointed friend. Dan glanced at Pip and his heart sank. For Pip avoided his look. Then, unbelievably, Pip turned and left them, his moccasins thudding softly on the causeway and over the bridge.

Billy Ben laughed good-humoredly. "Looks like your friend doesn't approve of us any more. Come on, let's go bye-bye." Halfway down the point road he broke into a cheery whistle. "Danny Boy." "—The pipes, the pipes are callin', From glen to glen and down the mountainside . . . 'Tis you, 'tis you, must go, and I must bide—"

Dan followed, fighting hard for control, and Caliban limped slowly along at his side. The boy could see all too clearly the black outcome of his plans. The tide would ebb. Locked in his room, he would be helpless to explore the causeway. Billy Ben, hard-driving, ruthless, missing nothing, would search the passage himself and find what there was to find. Then he would leave. Things would be little worse than they had been before, and Dan would be sent away from Pride's Point as if he had never come here at all.

When Dan looked back at the top of the road, he could see Pip just disappearing into the scrub on Oak Island.

And he saw in the east a great wall of fog, groping its blind way into the marsh.

CHAPTER EIGHTEEN

Last Warning!

~~~~~~

"I'VE got something unpleasant to report, sir." Billy Ben's sorrowful voice flowed on like an oily river. Dan heard himself accused. He saw his uncle's face grow stern, more sunken, like a skull's.

It might have been the very night Dan arrived. Then as now, he and Billy Ben had stood in the doorway, Uncle Julian by the fire. He had tried, he remembered, to say his thanks, and his uncle had failed to hear him.

Uncle Julian turned. There was sorrow in the handsome, high-born face. "Is this true, Dan?" He waited for the boy to deny it. "Dan. Dan. You gave your word—"

Billy Ben looked distressed, listening, listening.

Frantically Dan searched for words that would explain, without giving away the truth to Billy Ben. Time came to a stop.

Finally his uncle said heavily, "Your suggestion is a good one, Billy Ben. Get the key to Dan's room, please."

Billy Ben went off swiftly, soundlessly. Dan had a mo-

ment or two, that was all, to explain himself to his
uncle.

"I, too, was once locked in my room without supper, for
disobedience." The low voice sounded very tired. "But I
had not been disloyal to the family."

Stricken, Dan started to protest. But then Billy Ben
bulked in the door like a jailer. Uncle Julian turned away.
"I'll come up to your room later, Daniel. When I have
decided what you must do—" He whistled to Caliban and
the two, man and dog, disappeared into the office.

Dan followed Billy Ben to his room. He knew without
looking that the hired man wore a false smile of sympathy. The key was turned and left in its lock, then the light
footsteps disappeared down the hall. Now, as soon as the
tide was low, Billy Ben had a free hand at the causeway.

Fury choked Dan's throat and smarted in his eyes. He
wished desperately that the dog, at least, were with him
to share his imprisonment and disgrace. There was no
hope left from any direction. With nothing to wait for,
Dan settled himself at the window to wait.

Darkness began to fall and with it came the fog. It
came swiftly now, reaching into the marsh with white
tentacles, thickening even as he watched.

A movement below caught his eye. It was Billy Ben,
with a raincoat over his arm. He disappeared into the
carriage house and in another moment was backing out
the jeep.

Puzzled, Dan watched him out of sight toward the East
Marsh. This was likely nothing but a belated errand to
town, yet Dan felt a cold fear reach out of the fog. Surely

tonight Billy Ben would not leave the island before low
water without some special reason.

A frightening idea began to take shape. Billy Ben
needed ebb tide to examine the causeway and search for
the hideout. But he also needed time, plenty of time free
from interference. Uncle Julian planned to visit Dan's
room sometime later tonight. *So Billy Ben must clear the
field of Dan before the boy could talk to his uncle!* The
truth was so enormous that Dan was surprised he had not
seen it sooner. Somehow, Billy Ben must even now be
taking steps to get rid of Dan!

Dan paced the room. Here he was, locked up like a bad
child! The hired man's errand, already mystifying, now
became menacing. And there was no way to stop him.
Helpless and desperate, the boy stared out at the Bishop
house that rose hazily beyond Oak Island. Perhaps at the
causeway Pip had only pretended to be disappointed in
him. Perhaps he meant only to put Billy Ben off his guard.
Pip, come! Pip, come! he prayed.

Eight-thirty. In another half hour the tide would begin
to ebb. Perhaps Pip was even now in his room, watching
the darkness fall and the fog come in, watching the clock.
Pip had to be there! Dan could almost sense his friend's
impatience like a greeting across the marsh.

Like a greeting! Dan sprang from the window seat with
a surge of hope. He rummaged through his drawers for
his flashlight, praying that the fog was not yet too thick
for Pip to see his signal.

Quick, he would say. *Watch Billy Ben in York.* No need
to add *Important*. Pip would know it must be important,
if Billy Ben left the island now. In a sickness of impa-

tience, Dan cast back in his memory to camp days and the
Morse Code. First, the world *Quick*. What was Q? Yes,
dot, dot, dash, dot.

Over the marsh Dan flashed his message. *Quick. Watch
Billy Ben in York.* He sent it nervously, unevenly, three
times over. Then he waited. But there was no answering
signal. There was only the deepening dark, the swirling
fog.

Dan stood bleakly at the window. Pip would hardly be
sitting there, staring out at Pride's Island. Even if he did
see the message, what could the twins do to stop Billy Ben
without even knowing his plan? And if Billy Ben were
making only an innocent trip off the island, then the twins
would be sent on a wild goose chase, while the hired man
himself returned to explore the passage at his leisure!

These thoughts made sense. Yet, stubbornly, unrea-
soningly, Dan tried one last time. *Quick. Watch Billy Ben
in York.* He waited. The mist came in billows. It blotted
out first the house across the marsh, then the marsh itself,
and finally even the willows beyond the drive. Now there
was no need to watch any longer. The Fiddler's fog had
moved in. It had cut off the world with a curtain as solid
as doom.

Defeated, Dan slumped in the window seat for the
loneliest wait of his life.

He tried to study, then to read, and gave up both. The
hands of his clock crawled inchworm toward the hour,
and the old clocks struck faintly throughout the house.
Dan chafed in despair. With every slow minute the time of
low water was drawing nearer. And then the tide would

turn, would rise again and cover the entrance of the passage.

He heard the jeep return and, shortly after, watched Billy Ben move swiftly into the fog on his way down to the causeway. Then, for an age of waiting, there was nothing. Except that once, eyes straining, Dan thought he saw a slim figure move through the beeches below.

Moments later, steps came light and fast down the hall toward his door. A click in the silence like a gunshot: *the key, turned in its lock!* Then the genial voice, hushed now, reaching out of the gloom.

"There you go, Danny Boy, free as a dicky bird. Don't say I never did anything for you. Just give me time to get out of here—" A friendly chuckle. Quick cat steps on the stairs. Then nothing.

Dan did not move. But his mind raced uneasily from one course to another, like a dog seeking a scent. Had Billy Ben suddenly changed color, decided to help Dan? It seemed unlikely. Rather, for some reason of his own, Billy Ben wanted him free at this time, free and out of his room. Caution told Dan to stay where he was, do nothing.

On the other hand, whatever Billy Ben's plan, Dan might somehow find a way to explore the cave-in before Billy Ben himself did so. Perhaps, if he were to cut through the woods by the chapel—.

Dan caught up his flashlight and opened the door. The hall was dark and empty. Anxiously, he crept down the stairs. Billy Ben had left the great door ajar, like an invitation. The back yard was hazily lighted by an outside lantern. Dan hesitated in the doorway.

A figure detached itself from the black hall behind him.

Dan whirled. Then "Pip!" he cried gladly.

"No, it's me," said a shaking voice ungrammatically.

"Gilly?" Dan stared. The dark eyes looked enormous under the silly cap which covered her braids. Her nose was shining with perspiration. She looked frightened to death.

"I came to let you out, so you could explore the passage, if there is one. Only that b-baboon Billy Ben got here first—"

Dan drew her back, away from the doorway. She was shivering. "Take it easy, Gilly. What happened? Where's Pip?"

It all came out with a rush. "Pip's gone to York. He saw your signal just before the fog closed in. He told me about your plan to explore the cave-in tonight, and then how Billy Ben meant to have you locked in your room so you couldn't. He wanted me to help talk Mom into taking us to York to keep an eye on Billy Ben. But I wouldn't. I was— pretty mad."

Dan interrupted sharply. "They went, though?"

Gilly nodded. "Mom said she didn't know what good it would do in this fog. But she said Pip and I owed you this much, since you were in trouble on our account—"

"Go on."

Gilly drew a deep, uneven breath. "Pip got really mad with me. He said—he said I didn't even know the meaning of friendship. After they left, I got thinking about it and, well, here I am."

Dan looked at her in the gloom of the hall. In a Fiddler's fog, and at night, Gilly had taken the old road across the West Marsh. She had braved the bridge itself to help him!

"You know the meaning of friendship, Gilly," he told her.

She shook her head impatiently. "That's not all, Dan!" Her eyes grew darker still. "As I came over the bridge, there was Billy Ben working hard on the cave-in, moving stones away from it. He seemed strange, greedy, like something in a nightmare! Once he almost saw me, but I ducked down behind the stone rail. He kept listening for something—a car. Then you could hear it coming over the east causeway. He started up here as fast as he could. I thought of going home, but he looked—" Gilly hesitated, "well, evil. So I followed him here. And then, all he did was unlock your door." She broke off, breathless. "Is he maybe on our side after all?"

"No," said Dan.

"Then, what's it all mean?"

"I wish I knew," he said miserably.

"Dan," said Gilly, "go back! I've got this awful feeling— It's some sort of trap! Someone's heading out here, over the East Marsh. Maybe that's got something to do with it. Go back, and stay in your room!"

Dan stood torn between the need to get down to the causeway before the tide rose, and the wish to retreat to his room, to safety. He shook his head helplessly. "Where's the tide?"

Gilly thought. "Dead low, but knee-deep on Billy Ben at the cave-in. And it's about to turn."

Dan made up his mind. "Come along, we're wasting time."

He stepped out into the foggy night. With the girl just behind him he moved swiftly along the ell and around the main house. Then he stopped abruptly, a warning arm flung out.

Uncle Julian stood at the front door. He was talking with a man in uniform whose back was toward them.

"It's Johnny Lash," breathed Gilly in dismay.

Sick with defeat, Dan saw the patrol car in the driveway. So Pip had failed.

Uncle Julian was saying, "It couldn't possibly have been my nephew. Dan has been locked in his room all evening as punishment for—another matter."

"Do you mind if I see him, Mr. Pride," said Johnny Lash. It was an order, not a request.

"You're wasting your time, John, but come in if you insist. I'll take you up myself."

The door opened wider and light flowed across the lawn. Caliban limped to the doorway and sniffed the night air. Dan flattened against the wall and held his breath. A whistle from his uncle, and the dog moved reluctantly back into the house. The door closed.

"Something bad's happened," whispered Gilly. "They're blaming you, Dan!"

Dan stood silent, racked with indecision.

"It *was* a trap!" cried Gilly, stricken. "You've lost your alibi, unless you can get back to your room in time and let me lock you in—!"

Dan said desperately, "It's too late to go back. Hurry, will you, Gilly? They'll be after me soon enough."

They approached the causeway as Gilly had left it, crouched low and running softly. Once on the bridge, they flung themselves flat behind the rail.

Billy Ben, in a fever of excitement, was working with a crowbar. His breathing was heavy, and his face glistened in the circle of light. The tide had turned. It was above his knees now, but Dan drew a thankful breath. They were still in time! Now, to decide what to do—

Gilly was jubilant. She whispered, "See, Dan, he's making an opening right under the mooring rock—"

Dan put a frantic finger across his lips. But it was too late.

Billy Ben paused in the act of prising loose a stone. Dan and Gilly did not move. Surely in a moment he would continue. Surely they were still undiscovered, safe . . .

Billy Ben said, "Okay, Danny Boy. Come down from your perch, or I'll give you the crowbar—" He aimed the tool like a weapon and drew back his arm.

Gilly looked gray with anguish. Even as Dan moved to rise, she dug her fingers deep into his shoulder. Then she was scrambling down over the causeway toward Billy Ben.

"It's just me." Gilly was all innocence. "What's the matter?"

Surprised, Billy Ben lowered his arm. He narrowed his eyes at the figure in boy's jeans and cap. "I thought I told you to clear out," he said harshly. His keen eyes searched the bridge, and Dan went flat. "Where's your sister?"

Gilly! Gilly! warned Dan silently. *Tell him you're not Pip, and get away from here!*

"Gilly's home," said the girl carelessly. "I only came over to see Dan a minute."

Dan groaned silently. What was Gilly trying to do? Now Billy Ben would have to get rid of this unexpected problem. He was too close to his goal now, to leave anything to chance.

Billy Ben considered the heavy fog, thinking. He stood in front of Gilly, blocking her retreat to the bridge.

Gilly smiled trustingly. "What you doing anyway, fixing the cave-in?" It was Pip's voice and manner, as friendly and unsuspecting as a young dog.

Billy Ben hesitated. Then the menace fell away. "You said it. Been so busy lately, I have to catch up at night. How about that?" He smiled genially. He meant this boy to relax, to reveal whatever knowledge he might have of what lay beneath them here in the causeway.

Dan's thoughts all but burst out of him. *Gilly! He knows we're on to something. Don't act too innocent!*

Gilly crouched by the mooring rock and confided, "Listen. Dan thinks there's some old ruin down there. You found anything interesting?"

"Nothing but rocks and water," chuckled Billy Ben with relief. It was easy to read his thoughts: the Bishop boy was no threat. And Dan, about now, was running head-on into some real trouble—enough to keep him out of mischief for a while.

"Just what I told Dan," Gilly said guilelessly. "I thought I'd go up and see him for a minute. He must feel cussed low if they made him stay in."

"Can't be done," said Billy Ben cheerfully. "He's locked

in his room. And you better get back home before the dark shuts down."

Here's your chance! Go home, Gilly, go home! prayed Dan.

But Gilly was having too good a time playing her role. "Well, I'll just stick around a while with you," she said brightly. "Then, when his uncle's gone to bed, I'll sneak up and talk with Dan through the window."

It all came clear. Gilly was trying to keep Billy Ben from working on the tunnel! Gamely, she meant to make up for whispering and spoiling things.

Billy Ben's smile was broad and helpful. "Tell you what. You come up to my place and wait, and I'll let Dan out for a breather. His Uncle Julian won't mind a bit, since he won't know."

They laughed, two conspirators, but Gilly's laughter was high-pitched and tinged with hysteria.

Don't go, Gilly! This time he won't take any chances. He'll lock you up or something, and he'll talk his way out of it later on! Don't go!

His lantern high, Billy Ben came lightly, swiftly, up onto the causeway with Gilly behind him. Dan scrambled backward out of the range of the light. The girl was making a clatter to cover the sounds he made.

Billy Ben whipped around. "Keep it quiet, will you? Mr. Pride doesn't hold with night work. I'd get chewed out."

White-faced, Gilly nodded. She trudged firmly along beside Billy Ben. She did not once glance back at Dan. But the plucky set of her head seemed to say, "I got you into this, Dan, and now I've got you out. Get moving!"

Billy Ben's light bobbed eerily up the point and disappeared into the wet darkness. In a matter of minutes Johnny Lash and Uncle Julian would come looking for Dan. Minutes, and Billy Ben would be back. There was only a short time to act, and Gilly, brave little Gilly, had given it to him!

Dan leaped from his hiding place on the bridge and scrambled over the causeway to the mooring rock below.

CHAPTER NINETEEN

"Out of the Night—"

~~~~~~

DAN splashed hip-deep to the cave-in. Cautiously he turned on his light, and the beam lapped like fire into the causeway. Then he saw the reason for Billy Ben's excitement.

Just beneath the mooring rock the cave-in formed a natural barricade, now lowered by Billy Ben's efforts. Beyond it, Dan's light disclosed a narrow tunnel which disappeared into blackness!

Dan forget Johnny Lash, Uncle Julian, Billy Ben. Exultant, he eyed the opening. It might be possible even now to squeeze through to the opposite side! He was scrambling to the top of the barrier when he heard voices.

"There's the boy! Down to the river!" Then running feet, pounding on the point road. Lights, moving fast through the fog.

Dan stiffened. There was no time. He could be caught in the narrow opening like a rabbit in a trap. He switched off his light and thrust it high among the rocks. Then he was in the backwater, swimming fast and low for the Witches' Bridge . . .

Only when he reached the shadow of the third arch did he stop for breath. He clung to a rough stone and looked back. Three men were climbing down to the mooring rock, shining their lights toward the river. They looked ghostlike, yet as familiar as a nightmare. Their voices came clearly through the fog.

"He can't of gone far," said one.

"I heard him swimming. He won't get far swimming," said another. "Let's go."

Dan went cold inside. The men were lowering the skiff into the water. In a few minutes they would be here. They would search under the bridge, then down the river, along the banks where they could trace his passage through the salt hay beds of the East Marsh. Reason cried out that he had no chance against these local men and their lights.

Then instinct came to his aid. The West Marsh, with its sink holes and its hidden bogs—this they would leave till last. He might have time, if he had the courage, to find a hiding place there!

Dan stared with horror toward the steaming void to the west. Then he filled his lungs with air and began his flight, swimming underwater to Oak Island. There he kept to the black-grass, moving low like a hunted animal. By stops and starts, now running, now falling flat, Dan reached the rank grass that marked the beginning of the West Marsh. Here the thatch rose tall and coarse around him and he could safely walk upright. Slowly, the lights and voices fell behind.

He began to feel triumphant. The marsh and the night and the fog were all in league with him! With their help he had outwitted his enemies! Heady with victory he plunged on, away from Uncle Julian, and Johnny Lash and the men, on into the West Marsh.

For a time the turf seemed almost solid. But then the drowned earth began to suck at his feet. The glow from Pride's Island became lost in the fog, and darkness closed in. Then the sense of walking blindfolded into danger became strong and frightening.

The boy hesitated. Bella should be somewhere off to his right. He could faintly hear the river flowing through the vast wetlands that ranged to the west. Uncertainly, he moved on.

Once he plunged above the knees into a sink hole. He scrambled out in panic, snatching at the tussocks of coarse grass. After this he groped his way very slowly, hands outstretched, a foot questing always ahead like the antenna of a blind insect.

Once he stopped to listen, In that long moment, something dark and evil seemed to wait just beyond, or just behind.

Then panic drove him and he fled, running, running, the fear beating fast and heavy in his throat.

Suddenly the turf became greasy mud, then crumbled into nothing, and Dan plunged deep into chill water. Wildly his feet sought bottom. His hands clutched for grass, for sod. Nothing. He flung back his head and struggled to stay afloat. The black water rushed into his nose and mouth, and weeds tangled like a net around his body.

With the last of his strength he beat them back, thrashed at the water and the fear.

Then his feet touched mud, then nothing, then mud again. Weak with relief, he wrested himself up out of the slime. Then he lay still, choking for air, his cheek pressed against the muck, the black river licking at his feet.

In that moment he heard the motor. It was the *Jinx*, moving upriver, hunting him down. In the faint glow from their lights he saw that his refuge was the bank of the main stream where the marsh lay open and boggy and the grass grew scant. Dan looked about him in despair. To the south and toward the mainland, the marsh was more sea than land and offered little cover. And to the west lay Bella. But there on her rim the grass grew deep enough to hide a boy!

A chill wind stirred, and Dan hesitated. The wet glow of light was approaching the bend of the river. It was nearly upon him. Like a spent animal Dan crawled toward the salt pond. Here the very marsh seemed to quake. Now he was at the pond's edge, its ooze rising around him. Without warning, he plunged to the shoulder into its poisonous scum. Recoiling, he struck a rotted post, one of a circle of drowned staddles. He clung to these, knowing he could go no farther.

Bella. He saw at arm's length her black depths, steaming, evil. He felt on his body the insects which lived in her. He heard the oily bubbling of stagnant water and smelled the foul marsh gas. Yet here at the very edge of doom, the rotted sea bottom would still support him. So here, half-drowned and black with slime, Dan lay hidden.

The wet glow rounded the bend and illumined the

night. Close by, the heartbeat of the motor died. With aching eyes Dan peered through the grass and knew why the three men had seemed familiar. They were the firemen friendly with Billy Ben at the time of the grass fire on the point.

"He's gotta be somewhere," said a low voice. "Shine your light up that ditch there, Virgil."

The light changed direction.

"They's a million of them ditches," complained the man named Virgil. "Anyway, no kid's going to hide out in the West Marsh, not with the tide coming."

"He's in this marsh somewhere," said the man at the outboard, "and we'll find him, just like we found his raincoat outside the warehouse after the fire. And this time, that kid'll face a charge of arson."

The warehouse. After the fire. A charge of arson. A sick knowledge struck Dan. *Billy Ben had gone to the shipyard tonight and set fire to the warehouse!* It would have been an easy matter, one involving little risk. And he had left Dan's raincoat behind! Dan's reputation being what it was, they would have no choice now but to send him away. Dan began to shake, as if everything were already over.

The third man spoke. "Just suppose we don't find him."

"The time we get back, they'll have the rest of the Department out," said the man at the stern. "And we can always turn that critter Caliban loose. He'd scare up anything, I should think."

The third man said slowly, "I guess I was wondering if anybody'd *ever* find him."

"What do you mean?"

"Well, sir, here 'tis night, and the marsh, and a Fiddler's fog—the whole business. And that isn't all. I heard something back there by the bridge, when you fellers were putting the skiff over . . ."

"Heard what?"

"Well, it sounded like that fiddle they tell about."

There was an awed silence.

Then the man at the outboard laughed shortly. "Let's get going, or else they's no telling what we'll hear!" Hastily he started up the motor, and the skiff moved up river and out of sight into the fog-bound marsh.

Dan's neck ached. Wearily, he let his head fall back into the scum, and something sinuous whipped away from under his cheek. But he did not leave his hiding place. Not yet. In a moment he would go on, after he had thought . . .

The whole Department would be after him next, with their powerful searchlights. They would come into the marsh walking, with their hip boots on. They would come in boats, riding up and down the river, searching the creeks, the ditches. And then Caliban. If the men failed, then Caliban in his devotion would finally lead them straight to Dan . . .

The boy took a deep breath and prepared again for flight. The West Marsh had served its purpose. Now he would make his way straight back to the enemy, back to the tunnel. And there, if the entrance were not already under water, there he would hide.

On all fours, Dan made his way out of the salt pond. At each move of hand or knee, the ooze sucked hungrily after him. When he reached more solid ground he hesitated.

Which way was the sea? He was now too deep in the West Marsh to be guided by any glow from Pride's, and the choked waterways gave him no notion of direction. He dared not seek out the main creeks for fear of the men in the skiff. Yet, if he were to gain entrance into the tunnel before the tide sealed it off completely, there was no time to lose.

Then, faintly on his left, Dan heard a familiar sound. For an instant he was back at the Gut that first sunny afternoon with Pip. A piercing blast on a blade of fox grass. It sounded like the cry of a green heron, Pip had told him. There, it came again! And once again! Perhaps it was indeed a heron, calling out from the lost depths of the West Marsh. If so, he must not follow it.

But perhaps, perhaps it was Pip somewhere near the bridge, guiding him back.

He turned left, crawling fast through the salt grass, running low through the ditches with the brackish water up to his knees. And finally he saw the distant haze of light that marked Pride's Point.

Still unseen, Dan reached Oak Island. In the light of lanterns placed along the bridge, he saw two men standing guard. Even as he stared from the thick thatch, wondering how to reach the causeway, he heard the beat of a power boat from down river. The men hurried off the bridge toward the landing, waving their flashlights.

Dan moved as fast as his heavy limbs would allow him. He lowered himself into the river and swam from arch to arch to the opposite shore. Everything now depended on the tide. When he reached the pool he swam deep underwater, lest a chance kick yet betray him. Winded, he surfaced under the mooring rock, and peered anxiously at the drowned cave-in.

Only where Billy Ben had cleared the barricade, there remained the narrowest of openings! He could hear the tide washing over it into the passage beyond. Desperately he tried to picture the other side. The tunnel inclined upward, he remembered. But how much? Would there be room to breathe? If not, would he be able to make his way out of that dark trap in time?

His flashlight remained wedged above the tide-line. With a racing pulse, he hooked it onto his belt in order to free his hands for the trip into the tunnel. Then he heard the throb of the *Jinx* returning from the West Marsh. Quickly he forced himself through the opening. For a moment he clung to the barricade, felt wildly around for the bottom—and dropped.

He was inside the passage! Safe for the moment, Dan stood up to his shoulders in the chill water. A strange fulfillment came over him. He was standing at last in the escape passage built by Samuel's son. And surely his own grandfather had gone this way that last tragic night.

With a sense of wonder, Dan turned his back on the barricade. The scant light from the opening revealed a narrow passage which disappeared into blackness. The briefcase. It had to be somewhere in this weird hiding place. It had to contain proof of the Bishops' innocence, of Elder Corey's treachery . . .

Dan waded up out of the river. Here the tunnel floor was drifted with the black slime of the high tides; there it was cobbled like an early highway. He moved always upward, away from the glow at the entrance. Gradually the darkness, primitive and complete, closed down, and other senses came alive. The dank smell of underground. The slow drip of moisture from the rock, the wet sounds of his passage through the muck. Now and again the chill breath of the wind in the passage.

He unhooked his flashlight. He must use it sparingly, for if he found no way out it would be hours before the tide would allow him to return as he had come.

In its beam the ancient route, white-streaked with lime and moisture, sloped upward toward the chapel. Somewhere nearby, between the river and the chapel, perhaps beneath the chapel, must be the lost chamber!

He forgot his caution. He moved noisily up the tunnel, shining his light into every break in the stonework. At one point, a wall of bedrock loomed ahead, and here the tunnel turned sharply aside. Dan paused to examine the ledge, black, shiny with damp.

It was then that he heard it. He heard it surely, but without believing his ears. He heard the music of a violin! It began uncertainly like the wind. Then, swelling, it surged to the top of some mighty scale. High and vast it soared, filling the passage with sound that was both beautiful and terrible. Dan stood frozen, his light fallen, extinguished, forgotten. The music surged and resurged like a tide, and time stood blind and fearful.

Then the sound began to fade. It drew back down the scale to a long whisper, like the whining of the wind. With it, the terror drained out of Dan's mind, leaving it blank. Whatever was going to happen would happen now. He waited numbly in the darkness.

And a great voice spoke, filling the passage with echoes.

It was Samuel's curse, spoken thoughtfully as in a dream.

"*'Out of the night, and the fog, and the marsh, these three,*

Doom shall come for thee.'"

The voice sounded shaken by the music which still lingered in the passage. But it was familiar, and the chuckle was triumphant. It reached out of the shadows for Dan like a feeler, like Billy Ben's spotlight.

"Doom. How about that, Danny Boy? You ready for doom?"

Dan sucked in his breath. Then, dully, his mind began to work. Flat against the wall he moved into blackness, one vital step at a time. Billy Ben knew he was somewhere ahead. He had seen his light, heard his steps. Now he needed to know exactly where. He needed Dan to speak, to give himself away.

The light followed steadily behind him. The voice was nearer, panting a little, teasing. "How'd you like the music? You think 'twas me?"

Don't answer. Move only when he speaks. Move.

"Well, 'twasn't, and I never spoke a truer word. That was the Fiddler. Somebody's got trouble coming. You know who? You, Danny Boy. You."

Dan opened his mouth to protest. But Samuel's eyes looked fiercely out of the darkness. SILENCE! they said. SILENCE! said the eyes.

"Things look bad for you, Danny Boy. Liar. Traitor. Arsonist, it looks like. But hold on. Billy Ben's coming—" The glow steadied. Billy Ben stood listening.

SILENCE! Just so, Samuel had endured, had held his

peace. Not one fatal word had he uttered under the taunts, under the weights which crushed him.

"Lost your light, too, didn't you? Well, you wait right where you are. Here I come, light and all—"

SILENCE. One more careful step. Another. The side of Dan's sneaker touched something which started to roll. Desperately the boy firmed his foot against it. He stooped and closed an icy hand over his flashlight and moved on without a sound.

The soft footsteps came swiftly toward him and turned at the ledge. Light burst like an explosion into the boy's eyes. Billy Ben's stocky shape stood just behind it. And something else, something inhuman seemed to crouch just behind Billy Ben.

The beam rested full on Dan. Then it passed him, and the playful voice went soft. "And there's what we're both looking for. Take a look."

Beyond, the passage ended in a blank wall. In the circle of Billy Ben's light, several steps mounted to the vaulted roof and there ended.

"Can't have a kid running 'round talking," said the hired man, half teasing, half apologetic. "Not when there's a fortune to pick up and just the two of us to do it. Now can we, Danny Boy?"

Dan could not take his eyes from Billy Ben's light. It seemed that only the eyes and not the man at all were behind the glare, round and wide and innocent and bright.

"Anyway, you know what the Bible says? It says, 'Thou shalt not suffer a witch to live'." Billy Ben was moving swiftly toward Dan. He raised the heavy spotlight over his head like a weapon, and his great smile came clear.

Then, with a surprised cry, he whirled. The light spun

crazily round and round and smashed to the ground and went out. Dan, caught off balance, fell sharply against the wall. In that moment the night-black passage was filled with a brutal snarling and tearing, and the chilling sounds of human terror.

Dan scrambled to his feet. His flashlight was blind. The sounds mounted, then began to move away down the passage. Frantic, he shook his light and the beam flashed on. Just at the turn of the tunnel he caught a glimpse of familiar black fur, of white fangs. Caliban! Dan heard his own voice shouting, calling him off. But there was no stopping the animal. He was out of control, a devil with all his old hatred unleashed.

Dan ran down the passageway back to the river, his limbs like lead. There was splashing ahead, then silence.

The tide by now must have covered the entrance. But Billy Ben, like Caliban, was a fish in the water. Even now he would be swimming underwater, back up into the pool. He would think fast. He would say that he thought he had seen the boy in the river, and they would praise him for his courage. Then, later, he would come back to find the witches' chamber at the end of the stone stairs. And to find Dan.

There was no time to waste. Dan's forehead was bleeding. Impatiently he wiped it with his sleeve. His light was dim and he switched it off. Then, feeling his way back along the wall, he returned up the long passage.

Not even when the sound of the violin rose again, unholy and blood-chilling, not even then did he use his light. For even as the weird sounds swelled, even as he fought back panic, a strong damp wind fanned his forehead and he knew what the Fiddler was.

The wind, like Pan playing on a giant reed, was piping into the tunnel. *The Fiddler was the east wind!* Lamie was right. "Look for some natural cause," he said. The chill music mounted and soared. Then, gradually, it faded away. And through it all, the goodness of the old hermit kept Dan company to the end of the passage.

Only then did he use his light. Crouching on the top step, he saw that the vaulted roof was altered here by an area of flat stones. In this night of alarm and change, Dan was not surprised to see on one stone the clear mark of the double triangle. This would be the keystone! He pushed upward with all his strength. Painfully, with the cold sweat running into his eyes, he raised it. He slid it inch by inch over the stones alongside it, repeating the process until he had created a full-size trap door. And there, at last, was the true entrance to the passage, cunningly contrived and as everlasting as the rock itself.

Wearily, Dan pulled himself up through the opening. He played his light over a small room constructed of primitive stonework. *The witches' chamber!* he told himself in wonder. Several stone steps like those in the passage below climbed to a corner of the roof and to another trap door, opening, he was sure, into the chapel above.

Excitement rose in his throat. There was a table, a chair, a gasoline lantern. Against one wall stood a double file, and beside this, a small old-fashioned safe. Uncle Julian's unknown combination would fit it, surely! At last he was near the proof of the Bishop's innocence—or guilt.

The little room dipped, and telescoped. Dizzy, Dan sat down in the chair to think. He had something important to do. He must keep moving. He had to show them all how the wind entered the passage. Thus he could put to end forever the stories which had hagridden his family. And he had to show them this room, this safe, and the money sure to be in it. Then at last, the long feud would end between Prides and Bishops.

When finally he rose to his feet, he was surprised to find that his legs would scarcely support him. He was shaking with cold, as if he had been wrestling with his thoughts for a very long time.

In the waning glow of his flashlight he mounted the stone steps. With the last of his strength he forced the heavy stones aside and dragged himself up into the silent chapel. He sprawled shivering on the floor, more tired than he had ever been in his life.

Finally he replaced the stones in the floor. There was no mark to tell that anything at all lay beneath the chapel. Except—he looked closely—a faint triangle on the keystone of the trapdoor, all but hidden in the pattern of the floor!

He walked out into the night. The fog rolled past, salty and clean after the foul air of the witches' chamber. Dan wondered wearily about Billy Ben. Then he went down between the willows to the bright river.

The bridge and the point seemed to be peopled with half the town. The river glared with the headlights of cars parked on Oak Island and on Pride's.

Dan walked as far as the milestone before his courage and strength began to fail.

Then he stood unsure, scanning the strangers who faced the marsh as they talked quietly in groups. He did not see Uncle Julian, nor Pip. He felt exposed and vulnerable. All these people were looking for him. What should he say or do when they turned and saw him?

But nobody turned. Not ten yards away, he heard the quiet voice of Johnny Lash.

"I can't understand it. There's just no trace of the boy. You pretty sure you saw him in the river, Billy Ben?"

The men nearby stopped talking to listen.

"Sure as I'm standing here, Johnny. And if it hadn't been for that devil of a dog, I'd have had him, too. — Thanks again for pulling that critter off me."

"He better be kept chained up, a vicious dog like that," said Johnny Lash absently. "Just where did you say the boy was?"

"Right close to the bridge. Trouble is," Billy Ben added softly, "from the way he looked, I couldn't be sure he wasn't—"

"We know," Johnny Lash cut him off. "I guess we got to be ready for whatever we find. He didn't know these marshes—"

A boat throbbed its defeated, half-blind way back to the landing.

Johnny Lash sounded beaten. "I guess it's the grappling hooks next. Anyway, you tried. You really helped get things lined up here."

"Any time," said Billy Ben confidently. "Old Julian seems to be letting me take over, so I guess it's my job now. I'm a great one for planning, you know."

"I know." Johnny Lash turned wearily away. His gaze fell full on the muddy boy with the bleeding forehead who stood alone beside the milestone. He stared for a moment, startled.

As quick as a cat Billy Ben was beside Dan, his hand biting into the boy's shoulder. He was shouting something. Dan's name. "Here's our firebug, boys!" His hearty voice seemed to fill the lighted area from the point road to the bridge.

Dan did not move. He looked away from Johnny Lash, searching the faces which began to turn toward him. Everything went silent, as if the curtain had just risen on a great, fog-bound stage.

Then things happened fast. Yet, to Dan, they had the slow-motion pace of a nightmare.

Nearby on the bridge, a tall man standing apart moved clear of the shadows. Dan caught his breath sharply. It was Uncle Julian. He seemed ill and drawn, and he did not look at Dan. He merely stood listening, as if this was the end he had expected but would not watch.

Johnny Lash walked slowly toward Dan. He had the look of a man about to perform a sorry duty.

Then, before the officer could speak, a slight figure darted into the circle of light. It was Pip. He glanced at Dan and Johnny Lash, then at Billy Ben who somehow seemed to dwarf them both. Then impulsively, he turned to approach Julian Pride.

It was an incredible tableau. From the milestone Dan could see it vividly, framed by Billy Ben and Johnny Lash and the faces of strangers. There was Uncle Julian, aloof and unapproachable. Then Pip, moving anxiously toward him. And a third person, standing just at the edge of Dan's vision. It seemed to be Gilly, pale and grown up, and he knew at once that this was Ann Bishop.

Even as he stared, the picture changed. The woman

stepped back into the fog. Pip stopped. Julian Pride turned to face him, as cold as steel.

Pip said, "I'm Philip Cole, sir. Philip Bishop Cole."

There was not the slightest acknowledgement.

"Dan got in touch with me. He told me to go to York and keep an eye on Billy Ben."

Indignant, Billy Ben shouted something. Johnny Lash silenced him with a gesture.

Uncle Julian's face tightened as if he were thinking, "So the Bishops find it necessary to lie again."

Pip shuffled his feet but went bravely on. "My mother drove me there, and—"

Something passed over the frozen face and was swiftly gone.

"—And we saw Billy Ben down near the warehouse just before the fire. We saw him leave a raincoat there by the door, but we didn't know it was Dan's till now. We thought I better report it, sir, because Dan's getting blamed for something he didn't do."

"Something he didn't do!" The man looked down at the boy with scorn.

Pip cried, "But he couldn't have, sir! Not if he's been locked in his room!"

Julian Pride said without feeling, "Apparently he has not been in his room since late this afternoon." He looked bitterly around him. "You see these people, these cars. You hear the boats out in the marsh."

Pip nodded, white-faced.

"This search was organized so that my nephew could be found to answer to the authorities for the crime of arson. Although he has chosen to return of his own free will, he will not remain at Pride's Point. Therefore, you need not come here again."

Pip stood helplessly, with no words left. Ann Bishop, chalk-white at the edge of the shadows, remained silent. Julian Pride bowed his head against the lights in his eyes, and started off the bridge.

Johnny Lash sighed. "Come on, son," he said to Dan. "Unless there's something you want to say first."

Dan could not have uttered a word in his defense. Watching Uncle Julian, he found that he no longer cared. He was shivering uncontrollably from a chill that came from deep inside him.

But Billy Ben gave a short, triumphant laugh. "Well, just for the record, I've got something to say! The Bishop kid's lying all right, and I never spoke a truer word! Johnny Lash can come up to my cottage and see the proof for himself—a smashed window, or a busted lock—"

Johnny Lash's eyes were steady and sharp. "How come?"

"Because a while back, I found the kid snooping around this property, probably over here to turn Dan loose. I'd already warned him once about trespassing. So this time I took him up to my place and locked him up till Mr. Pride could see to him. Only with all the hue and cry after Dan, I clean forgot him. You can see for yourself he's busted out, bold as brass and still lying—"

Suddenly the ice inside Dan broke up. The words poured out, cold and fluent. "Pip didn't break out of your cottage, Billy Ben, because you never shut him up in the first place. You talked with Gilly, his twin, and locked *her* up. Pip was in York all right, and if he says he saw you at the warehouse, he saw you there."

Billy Ben turned and stared at Dan. Slowly his face went dark red. He started to curse, and his voice was rough and loud.

But there was no stopping Dan now. "And just before that, after you returned from York, you came to my room. You unlocked my door so that I'd have no alibi for the fire. But you see, Gilly was there in the hall. She saw you."

Billy Ben's head thrust forward like an angry bull. His hands knotted into great fists. He was thinking lightning fast.

Swiftly Ann Bishop spoke up. Her words were low, but very clear. "Dan is right. Whether Julian Pride believes this or not, my son and I were in York tonight. We did see Billy Ben at the warehouse, just as Pip has told you—" Her voice went soft. "And knowing Gilly, I'm sure she came here as Dan has said, and must still be at the cottage. Surely her word, too, will be enough—"

With a vicious thrust, Billy Ben sent Dan reeling into Johnny Lash and the group of men standing nearby. There was the dash of footsteps across the bridge into the fog.

Then the stage turned into a nightmare of outcry and pursuit. A confusion of men shouting and running. Spotlights turned onto the river, onto the bridge, into the wilderness of Oak Island. On one side Dan saw Pip and his mother, with one of the men, hurrying up to Billy Ben's cottage. On the other, he saw Johnny Lash start toward the bridge with an order.

The policeman remembered Dan briefly. "No time to

say this now, son," he called back, "but we're sure sorry. And don't worry. We'll get him."

There was too much for Dan's tired head to take in. He leaned weakly against the milestone.

A tall shadow detached itself from the group milling on the causeway and walked unsteadily toward the boy. Through a mist of helpless tears Dan saw his uncle bend. He felt the hard arms go about his shivering body. He felt the stern face wet against his own. And all at once, Dan knew he had come home.

CHAPTER TWENTY

The Tide Goes Down

~~~~~~

THE new day began as the night had ended, chill and bleak, with the fog blotting out town and marsh alike. But early in the morning came a change in the air. The wind shifted into the west and promised at last a fine warm day and a blue sky.

Like the wind, the talk in the town was changing. For the first time in their lives, the good people of York shook their heads and wagged their tongues over their own misdeeds, rather than those of the Prides.

Johnny Lash did his best to answer the questions that sped like gulls over the town that day. How Billy Ben had set fire to the warehouse to involve young Dan Pride. How young Dan, fleeing the false charge of arson, had hidden in the West Marsh. How half the town had turned out to hunt him down like a criminal. And then how the boy's safety had become, for part of an anxious night, the chief concern of the town.

"Wonder how Billy Ben ever come to do a thing like

that," said one, leaning against the wall of the drug store.

"Easy," said another. "The shipyard wasn't good enough for him. He figured on taking over at Pride's sooner or later, I know from the way he talked. And if young Dan hadn't come and spoiled the picture, he would have, too, 'specially with Julian Pride getting sort of queer—"

"Don't know but what I'd get queer myself, living out there alone in the marsh," said the first. "And then you take all that foolishness about the Fiddler—"

But Johnny Lash shook his head. " 'Twasn't foolishness, Folks really heard that fiddle music all these years. —Only the boy's laid that ghost, for good."

Heads looked up. "How come?"

And the story was told, as it would be told many times in the days to come, of the long-forgotten witches' passage in the causeway, and how when the tide was right, you could hear the weird music of the east wind in the tunnel.

The men thought this over.

"They going to press charges against Billy Ben?"

"That'll be kind of hard, since he's cut and run," said Johnny Lash dryly. "Anyhow, that old warehouse didn't amount to a hill of beans, and Ann Bishop never did like trouble. Billy Ben'll get off with a scare and a warning—if he ever comes back."

"He's got Pride's Point in his blood," said the first. "He'll be back sooner or later, even if he has to look at it from down river."

The Boston bus blared around the corner, slowed down

in front of the drug store, then picked up speed and roared off into the thinning fog. The men looked soberly after it, busy with new thoughts.

And the life of the town went on, but not quite the same as before. Late in the morning the sun broke through at last and burned down over marsh and sea alike. And the tide began to run out of the marshland, out of the creeks and the streams and the ditches. Once again, the broken entrance to the ancient passage was coming free.

Across the East Marsh in the old room in the gable, Dan slept until the sun fell full upon his face. The chill of last night was gone, and he felt warm and peaceful. He lay for a happy moment, counting his aches and bruises like battle scars; remembering the talk he had had with his uncle until the fire burned low and daylight filled the windows, and everything had finally been said between them.

Then he was out of bed, for vital things were about to happen. He had nearly finished dressing when Mrs. Corey, red-eyed with sleeplessness, appeared at his door.

"*Clean* socks," she said. Her voice was curt to hide her feelings.

"Yes'm." Dan hastened to obey.

"That phone's been ringing something turrible!" complained the housekeeper. "First it's your Uncle Julian and Johnny Lash, chewing the rag; then it's half the town, wanting to find out how you are, and everything else that's none of their business. Now it's those Bishop young ones again."

Dan looked up, grinning. So Pip and Gilly had braved the phone and called Pride's Point!

"Your uncle left word you can call 'em back soon as you're up. He even said you might like to show 'em that passage, soon as the tide gets down," she added grudgingly.

Dan tried to hide his pleasure. Perhaps Uncle Julian had at last had a change of heart toward the Bishops! Then he sobered, realizing that the hatred of years would not so easily end. His uncle had misjudged Dan and was granting this favor to show it. Nothing more.

"He says to meet him in the chapel at noon. He's gone into the city to get something out of his safe deposit box, he said."

Dan nodded, his pulse hammering. The combination. Soon, success or failure, they would know the contents of the safe in the hidden room!

"Use the phone in the library and don't talk all day," she told him sharply. "I been waiting breakfast long enough." Then she studied his face, the cut on his forehead, and her eyes misted with honest affection. "You all right, Dan? Billy Ben didn't touch you, did he?"

Dan shook his head, not knowing what to say.

"He fooled me, too," she said shortly. "I guess he fooled us all." She looked beyond him toward the Witches' Bridge. "He got away, you know," she added thankfully. "Only he won't ever be happy, away." She plodded down the hall and Dan followed silently.

Dan's call to the Bishops was a lengthy, three-way

conversation, with Pip and Gilly stationed at separate phones in the house across the marsh. Twice Mrs. Corey stuck her grizzled head into the library. The third time she planted her hands on her hips and loudly recited the menu: "Blueberries'n cream; sausages; scrambled eggs *and* hot muffins. All getting cold."

"I'll meet you at the mooring rock," Dan told the twins hastily. "Twenty minutes."

In even less time Dan was taking the short cut across the field to the point road. The sun thrust hot through the fog and turned the world into a dazzle of light. It struck fire from the lilacs and touched the lawns with brilliance. Billy Ben's gardens glowed with colors rare even in the marsh. But they would never again feel his special care.

Dan glanced at the chapel as he passed. Billy Ben would never now fill in the trench along the old foundation. On the other side of the road the orchard, laden with young green apples, sloped sunny to the marsh. Someone else would gather this year's harvest, and Dan would not hear again the cheerful, false notes of "Danny Boy" across the fields of Pride's Point.

His father had once said: "A person is only as good as he is able to be." Perhaps Billy Ben wasn't able to be any better than he was.

Caliban joined him, loping in his painful gait from the barn. He pressed against the boy with little moans of pleasure. Dan fondled his ears, and they went on together down over the causeway, just as Pip and Gilly ran from the green shadows of Oak Island.

Pip brought his thumb and forefinger together in a

blithe greeting that said, "Well done!" And Gilly ran up anxiously, her braids flying. "Are you all right, Dan?"

"You look pretty good," said Pip with relief. "Except for that mess on your head."

"I'm fine." Dan was suddenly self-conscious, unsure of what to say.

Gilly said with surprise and a touch of shyness, "I hadn't noticed, but you're most as tall as Pip now."

Awkwardly they clambered down to the mooring rock. Pip went on his knees and peered over the edge. The water lapped only inches beneath his nose.

"Just look at this cussed tide," he chafed.

"Keep calm. We can squeeze in pretty soon," comforted Gilly.

Dan surveyed the opening. "A matter of minutes," he said. His eyes darkened as he remembered the last high tide at this place.

Gilly settled herself on the mooring rock and gazed with awe at the West Marsh. "One thing you didn't tell us over the phone, Dan," she said slowly. "How did you find your way alone out of that horrible West Marsh, at night and in the fog?"

"I didn't. I'd very likely be there yet, except for Pip and his fox grass."

Pip grinned with delight. "You heard me? By golly, I knew you'd hear me. When we got back from York we tried to contact Johnny Lash and finally traced him here to Pride's. Then we learned you were out in the marsh, and I figured you could use a little guidance. I had quite a while to think about it, too. Johnny Lash was all tied up with Lamie, and Mom refused to—bother your Uncle Julian."

Dan brightened. "Lamie? He was here?"

Pip nodded. "Your uncle and Johnny Lash sent for him. He told them lots more places to look. He sure knows the marsh!" Then he added, "He didn't like all the commotion. But he looked sort of peaceful, as if he knew things would still turn out okay."

"And I had to miss him *again!*" wailed Gilly.

Pip grinned at his sister. "Right then you were trying to hammer down Billy Ben's cellar door. You should have seen her, Dan, when we got up there. She looked a mess. All red in the face, and—"

"I did not!"

"Gil looked great. Sounded even better. They say with a voice like hers she'll make the cheering squad hands down, next year."

"Huh," said Gilly, pleased.

Dan said thoughtfully, "If it hadn't been for Gilly, I should never have reached the passage before Billy Ben. And if it hadn't been for you, Pip, I should still be considered guilty." He stared at the great old chimneys beyond them. "Well, the old score is settled, don't you think?"

"Sure thing," Pip said easily. "And there won't be any more witch hunts, either."

Gilly mused, "Mother says people in town are feeling pretty much ashamed of themselves. Billy Ben made fools of them, and they don't like it. They'll make up to you and your uncle somehow, Dan. You just see if they don't . . ."

Abruptly Pip dropped with a splash into the backwater,

jeans and all, with the river up to his chest. Gilly joined him, heedless of clothing. Together they peered into the barricade.

"Let's go!" Pip said.

Dan stared down at them from the mooring rock. Suddenly he wanted less than anything on earth to go up that passage today. The answer to everything lay inside the little hidden room. The money had to be there in the safe!

But supposing it was not?

Reluctantly, he lowered himself into the ebbing tide as the twins climbed through the opening.

Tight-lipped, Gilly was the first to let herself down into the twilight on the other side of the wall. The boys and the dog followed with a muffled splash.

In the beam of Dan's flashlight the three waded up the passage out of the dark tide. Caliban swam beside them; then, nose to the cobbles, ranged beyond as if he had often been this way before. The twins gaped at the arched tunnel, the dripping blackness ahead.

"This took nerve, Dan," said Pip with respect. "You couldn't have known whether you could get out either way—"

Gilly cleared her throat. "Smells like a grave, doesn't it?"

"I wouldn't know," said her brother too loudly. His voice went echoing down the narrow tunnel.

Dan led the way, with the twins close to his heels. The streaked walls closed in on them, and the smell of age and mold.

"When do we reach the end?" whispered Gilly.

"Soon enough," Dan told her. Too soon. Uncle Julian

might already be there in the hidden chamber. He might already have opened the safe, already have found it empty. If only the trouble and mystery could have ended out there in the sun. Instead, the old tale must come to a finish in its own grim way, here underground like the work of the devil.

Suddenly the black ledge loomed before them. Gilly made a sound of dismay.

"It's all right. The passage turns—" Dan whispered. He stopped. For a sick instant he heard again the eerie music, and saw the hulking shape of Billy Ben.

"We lost or something?" asked Pip, concerned.

"What's the matter, Dan?" said Gilly in a tight voice.

"It was just here I heard—the music," said Dan unwillingly. "And Billy Ben came—"

"Look," said Pip in a low voice. "There's Billy Ben's flashlight, busted all to bits."

The twins stared. Here was proof of the force behind the hired man's intended blow.

"Dan," said Gilly with horror, "he meant to—"

"I know," said Dan. Yet, for a moment, he smelled again the sweetness of new-cut hay in the East Marsh and felt the burning of the July sun. He heard the burst of Billy Ben's laugh above the chug of the tractor, and saw his face flushed and friendly against the sky.

"If it hadn't been for Caliban—" Pip said with awe. "He must have really hated Billy Ben."

The dog had come back to them. He thrust his cold nose into Dan's hand. Later Dan would tell them why the dog hated Billy Ben. Just now he could not think any more about the old hatreds at Pride's Point.

Suddenly time seemed short, and Dan moved swiftly

on. Then they were at the tunnel's end, at the stone stairs
that climbed to the roof. Together the boys inched the
slabs onto the floor above, and helped Gilly up through
the opening. Dan caught a glimpse of Caliban as he
limped out of sight back down the tunnel. As naturally
as if he were crossing the road to the barn, the dog would
make his way back to the cave-in, and out into the sun.

They replaced the stones. Then the twins stood shivering beside Dan in the hidden room, fascinated by what
they saw: the symmetry of the musty chamber, the
cleverly-fitted trap door with its ancient steps secreted
beneath their feet; the matching stairs that mounted the
opposite wall; the sparse furnishings; the moldering file.
The safe.

Gilly cocked her head like a startled robin. "What's
that?" she whispered.

It came again. A ghostly rapping on the stone that sur-
rounded them. It seemed to spring from everywhere.

Then Dan understood. The sound came from the chapel
above. "It's Uncle Julian," he said, "with the combination
to the safe." In a few minutes they would know, for better
or worse, the final answer.

The twins stared anxiously at Dan. They all shared the
same grim thought. Pip put the thought into words.

"What if the money isn't here?"

"I don't know," said Dan. "I don't know."

Slowly, with Pip behind him, he climbed the steps. He
reached for the center stone above his head just as the
stone itself was thrust aside.

Dan's heart twisted, for the face above them was familiar and beloved, eager, almost boyish. It was, for a moment, the face of Dan's father! As the two pairs of dark

eyes met, understanding flickered between them and burned steadfast. In the time it took Julian Pride to enlarge the opening and climb down beside them, Dan knew one thing surely. It need not matter now, too much, what they found in the safe!

Julian Pride scanned the chamber swiftly, included the twins. His glance returned to rest on Dan.

Dan waited tensely. Prides and Bishops, together. But the bitter look did not come.

"We timed our meeting well," said Uncle Julian. "Now let's see whether this combination works."

He squatted on his heels before the safe. Unconsciously Dan moved close beside him. They watched together, Prides and Bishops, as Julian Pride spun the dials, then swung open the steel door.

Inside were several air-tight containers. Wedged on top of these was a small leather case, gray with mold.

Julian Pride hesitated. Then he took out his father's case, opened it, examined its contents. Stiff with suspense, Dan did not once take his eyes from that thin face.

Finally his uncle looked at Dan. The eyes were black and haunted. Dan's heart fell. His uncle had gone into that other world with his misery and his hatred, leaving Dan behind. The case must contain, then, only receipts, documents. No money. No proof of the Bishops' innocence.

Then, softly, Julian Pride spoke. "Yes. He came back here with the money. Father never paid Philip Bishop one cent of it. He never reached their house at all that night."

Dan drew an uneven breath.

"You were right, Dan. Elder Corey must have followed him onto the bridge to rob him. Then Father escaped to this chamber of his and hid the money, here with his records. Elder Corey—" He spoke the name as if he were saying it for the first time.

"Lamie heard him, and saw his light," said Dan hoarsely. "There's no proof, really, just a great lot of little things. Most of all, Billy Ben *knew,* you see. *Someone* had told Billy Ben that the money never left Pride's!"

Uncle Julian looked at his nephew without seeing him. "I should have guessed. Billy Ben was searching for this all along." His voice was filled with wonder. "Elder Corey. Not the Bishops. Never the Fiddler."

Dan heard a small, relieved sound from Gilly, or from Pip. He felt a dark weight slipping from his mind.

When Uncle Julian stood up he seemed taller than ever, so straight was he standing. His voice was sad, but firm. "Do you know what this means? It means I have been mistaken for a long time, longer than you three have been alive." He looked at Gilly and Pip.

Then he went on slowly, as if it cost him a great deal to say the words. "And it means I have done a great wrong to others—and must somehow make amends."

He closed the safe and continued briskly, "You're all shivering. I shall take the briefcase and invest the money properly. And if you are interested, we'll all come back tomorrow and look through the old records. In time, I expect, most of these things will go to the local museum."

Caliban met them at the chapel door. The sun, arcing toward high noon, had all but dried his wet coat. Now it warmed the chill out of the four who stood together in the clearing.

Billy Ben's trench gaped raw and dark in the shadow of the wall. For a few moments they stood in silence. There would be days and years ahead for all their thoughts to be shared. Yet there was one thing, one unbelievable fact, that Dan knew he could never share. Except for Samuel Pride, the witch, Dan could not have kept silent in the witches' passage last night. How it had happened Dan did not know. But it had happened. If it had not, things would have turned out very differently.

Dan had a thought. "Lamie. Lamie ought to be told about the passage and the witches' chamber!"

"Here's an idea," said Uncle Julian, as if it had just occurred to him. "Why don't you and the twins invite Lamie to lunch, and take it with you to his island, where he feels at home?"

"That's a great idea, sir!" exclaimed Pip. "We already have our swimsuits on. All we have to do is go home and grab some sandwiches—"

"As it happens, Mrs. Corey has a picnic lunch already packed for four," said Uncle Julian. "She promised a rather special one."

"Four? You coming too—sir?" asked Pip uncertainly.

"The fourth will be Lamie, I expect," said Uncle Julian. Dan was not certain, but he thought he saw a twinkle in his uncle's eyes.

Gilly blurted, "I wish you'd come too, Mr. Pride!"

Uncle Julian looked at her in surprise. Then he said, "Thank you. Will you ask me another time?"

The girl nodded shyly.